SCAPEGOAT

SCAPEGOAT

James Rhys Roberts QGM

CPW BOOKS.
Columbia Publishing Wales Limited

First Published in the UK in 2002 by:
COLUMBIA PUBLISHING WALES LIMITED.
Glen More,
6, Cwrt y Camden,
BRECON LD3 7RR.
Powys, Wales. UK.
e-mail mail@columbiapublishing.co.uk

Copyright © James Rhys Roberts.

The right of James Rhys Roberts to be identified as the author of this work has been asserted by him in accordance with the Copyright Designs and Patents Act of 1988.

All rights reserved.

A CIP catalogue record of this book is available from the British Library and The National Library of Wales.

ISBN 0-9538945-1-7

The moral right of the author has been asserted.

All rights reserved. No part of this publication may be reproduced, stored in a retrieval system, or transmitted at any time or by any means electronic, mechanical, photocopying, recording or otherwise, without the prior permission of the publisher.

This book is sold subject to the condition that it shall not, by way of trade or otherwise, be lent, resold, hired out, or otherwise circulated without the publisher's consent in any form of binding or cover other than that in which it is published and without a similar condition including this condition being imposed on the subsequent purchaser.

Printed and Bound in Wales.
By: Creative Print and Design Wales,
Ebbw Vale NP23 5SD.

ACKNOWLEDGEMENTS.

The Furey's 'Green Fields of France.' By E. Bogle {Sonet Publishing}

Dedication.

To My Boys; Robert, Ian, James, John and Jake Rhys.

' For You The World.'

CHAPTER ONE

'Up eight hundred feet, four men jumping', shouted the RAF PJI.

'Eight hundred, four men jumping', replied the RAF corporal operating the mechanical winch that would allow the dopey, tired-looking, grey barrage balloon to ascend from the earth. The cage suspended beneath the balloon rocked as it reluctantly left terra firma. The five occupants held firmly onto the sides of the cage to steady themselves.

Ralph Ellis looked around the cage at his fellow parachutists and the wiry old RAF jump-instructor who stood at the gate. He being of the old school, there would be no straying from the drills hammered into the students at the Parachute Training School; not today. The balloon ascended gently, at about one hundred feet above the ground all was quiet, not a word spoken. Ralph studied the young corporal standing opposite him sporting the American wings on his chest. In Aldershot circles, this badge was known as 'The Flying Ice-cream'. The corporal was trying his best to appear brave but was betrayed by the greenish grey tinge, which gradually suffused his cheeks as the balloon gained height. The other two members of this jolly crew were, without doubt, recruits. The red epaulettes of the Advance Platoon showed under their parachute harnesses and they made no effort to conceal their nervousness. After the initial turbulence as the balloon left the ground, most had now relaxed their grip on the side of the cage, except the two recruits who still hung on for dear life.

Someone farted.

'Chicken vindaloo if I'm not mistaken', quipped the RAF PJI, comically sniffing at the air.

'More like essence of adrenaline', quipped Ralph.

This bout of badinage, both verbal and anal, seemed to relax the atmosphere. Both recruits attempted false smiles, and the corporal even managed to speak.

'Staff, do you think we'll jump? The wind seems to be gusting'

'Yes, I can smell it', replied the PJI, smiling. 'But don't worry, you'll go, I'm not suffering your backside all the way back down that's for sure'.

The Corporal did not appear to be impressed by this news; the recruits managed a sly smile at each other.

'You've been doing this almost as long as I have haven't you Ralphie?' The PJI turned Ralph.

'Yes, but not for much longer. A quick four this morning will be my last'. There was sadness in Ralph's reply.

'You will be lucky to get four in this morning mate. That new DZ officer is watching like a hawk; cost cutting and all that'. The PJI looked down at the blue flat cap some distance below.

'Typical', added Ralph. 'When you want to do some they won't bloody let you'.

The balloon was now approaching eight hundred feet above

SCAPEGOAT

Queens Avenue, the vast green of the various sports pitches spread out below them. The wind, as the Corporal had correctly pointed out, was gusting, causing the balloon to sway back and forth. In fact as the balloon ceased its ascent the cable to the ground was at a dangerously acute angle. The balloon was over the Farnborough Road, which bordered the DZ.

'That's it off then?' offered the corporal, almost in desperation.

'No such luck, we've got a green flag'. Ordered the PJI.

'Shit!' Muttered the corporal, almost to himself.

The PJI reached forward and pulled the metal pin which secured the metal bar, 'the gate', from the cage.

'Right, there's going to be no fucking about! We're drifting on and off the DZ. When I say go, you GO!' The PJI had raised his voice at the appropriate time. It was time for business, and he meant business.

'Number One, come forward, hands on the door'. The corporal staggered forward.

'When I shout go, push forward, make sure you clear the sill'. The corporal nodded acknowledgement.

Ralph was looking over the side of the cage into the distance. Over the years he had thrown himself out of balloons, helicopters and aircraft many times. He was one of the few members of the Parachute Regiment who actually enjoyed parachuting, especially balloon descents, which were generally hated by all. After today there would be no more debating whether one of the rugby posts left standing on the playing fields would work it way up your jacksie. He would have more important things on his mind soon, like paying the council tax or mowing the lawn. The thoughts of civvy street frightened him more than any parachute jump.

The smell of vindaloo drew Ralph's attention again as the PJI ordered,

'Standby, GO!'

The corporal turned his head towards the PJI as if to ask confirmation. He got it, the PJI pushed him firmly out of the exit, the odour followed him tumbling unceremoniously towards earth.

'Knob'. Said the PJI, almost casually as he turned back to face the remaining passengers.

'Right, number two'. He addressed the nearest recruit in a reassuring manner. The recruit followed the shining example of his mentor and made his way forward, grabbing the sides of the basket nervously as he went.

'We're not going to have to have a repeat performance of that, are we?' the PJI said into the ear of the recruit.

'No Sir!' replied the recruit, promoting the Staff Sergeant, just slightly.

'We have a Green, Standby, GO!' The PJI commanded. The recruit took off, his arms came quickly across his chest as his hands gripped the sides of the reserve parachute.

'That's better!' Rejoiced the PJI, aiming his comment at the remaining recruit.

'Number three, let's have you.' Gesturing to the recruit to come forward, a big smile on the face of the PJI.

The recruit made his way forward gingerly and took up the required position at the exit. Ralph had drifted off again, he had been wondering off into daydreams regularly since his redundancy had been confirmed. Now his mind was back on Weston on the Green, and his first parachute jump some eighteen years ago. He could clearly see himself as a recruit, waiting his turn to enter the balloon cage. Remembering the

SCAPEGOAT

friendly abuse he had shouted at his mate Andy Woods, as he entered the balloon cage two groups ahead of him. He looked up as he recalled the deafening twang as the cable securing the balloon had snapped. Luckily the sudden rocking of the escaping monster had thrown the occupants clear. But Andy had broken his ankle in the fall. This resulted in his mate being put back in training and arriving in the Parachute Battalion several months after him. Over the years they were to go in separate directions, but the friendship remained. Andy was one of the few people that Ralph knew he rely on even though he had seen little of him since he had passed SAS selection and joined the 'Regiment', as it was known. He had invited Andy to his Dining Out dinner tonight, but had received a vague 'not available' message from Hereford.

'Go!' Shouted the PJI, bringing Ralph abruptly back to the present. The second recruit, like the first, did everything asked of him. Leaving the two old contemptibles waffling in the cage as if they were standing on a railway platform at Waterloo.

'You'll miss all this Ralph, what you got planned for civvy street?' Enquired the PJI.

'Copper, what else. There's no call for marksmen on the general purpose machine gun nowadays'. There was no enthusiasm in Ralph's words.

'See you tonight then mate, off you go'. The PJI said casually.

'Warmers in the bank, half past six in the Rat Pit'. Ralph said over his shoulder as he stepped from the balloon cage.

Ralph didn't need to be shouted at, he had seen the DZ Officer waving the green flag to show the all clear. He intended to enjoy this descent, it could be his last one. Especially if he failed to bluff his way back into the queue for the next balloon. He didn't count to ten [cliche?], as they were taught nowadays, just threw his head back and watched the chute deploy. If there was anything wrong with it he would notice it immediately. All was well as his body fell backwards as he descended, he could see the steel balloon cable some distance away from him. His boots appeared in front of his face just before the deploying parachute filled with air and acted as a giant air brake causing him to swing backwards. This must be one of the best feelings in the world, he thought to himself. He assessed his drift and noticed the ambulance racing across the DZ to attend to one of the others who had gone before him. He selected his front lift webs, reached high and pulled down hard in an effort to slow his landing speed. This wasn't going to be a picnic the wind was changing direction every second. The ground was rushing up to meet him [with a bump], he was sure he was on the wrong lift webs but sod it, too late now. Ralph was breathing in short gasps, pregnant woman style, as he hit the ground. Any plans for a final stand up landing were out of the window. He was thrown heels, arse and head backwards and then unceremoniously dragged along the ground for half a football pitch. He quickly screwed his body round, jumped to his feet and ran around the chute causing it to collapse.

'Do I really want to go through that again?' he asked himself.

'Yes, of course I do,' was the answer.

He quickly rolled up the used parachute and crammed it into the green bag he had been given, attached the unused reserve chute to the handles of the bag and threw the lot over his shoulder heading for the winch lorry. He heard someone shouting, initially he ignored it but eventually turned to face the

SCAPEGOAT

culprit.

'Who are you then?' Asked the young RAF DZ Officer.

'Colour-Sergeant Ellis, 2 Para, Sir', Ralph shouted back confidently hoping it would help in his effort to justify his presence.

'This programme is for Depot personnel only, why are you here Colour Sergeant?'

'No excuse Sir, just keen'. Ralph replied.

'Well go and be keen somewhere else, we are on a strict budget these days, you should know that.' the DZ Officer added as Ralph turned to walk away.

'Fucking crabs!' Muttered Ralph.

'What was that Colour?' Enquired the Officer.

'I think I've got crabs, Sir', Ralph replied theatrically scratching his groin.

'I'm sure you have Colour, I'm sure you have'. The DZ Officer said as he gave up and walked away in the opposite direction.

Ralph also admitted defeat and threw the green bag in the back of the RAF lorry. Then it hit home. It really was the last time, never again would he enjoy the experience, the fear. Fear was the common denominator of the Airborne Forces. Whatever the rank, whether you had been educated at Eton or Aspley Secondary School, as Ralph had, when it came to parachuting all experienced the same fear, the same apprehension. Peace time parachuting had it's safety limits when it came to wind speeds, but when a Commanding Office had eight Hercules C130 aircraft packed with troops his thoughts were not of safety limits. The result was often hospitals full of broken bones and ruined careers. Ralph had been lucky, not skilled. No one was skilled at military parachuting, you were either lucky or

JAMES RHYS ROBERTS

injured. Perhaps now was the time to go, while the going was still good. He consoled himself with this thought as he walked from the DZ.

CHAPTER TWO

'Rap, Rap, Rap!' sounded the gavel at the end of the long shiny mahogany table. It had been a good meal, the Beef Wellington had been Ralph's choice. A privilege always reserved for the person who was leaving the Sergeants Mess, the unit or in Ralph's case, the Army.

There was a good turn out. Virtually all the Mess Members were present, all dressed in their immaculate red coloured jackets, except for a few attached personnel in their unit uniform. The dining room was steeped in history. Original paintings depicted gliders landing at Arnhem and silver statutes of past heroes of the Regiment charged pillboxes and the like. The long tables were adorned with silverware ranging from cigar boxes to candelabra, all burnished for hours before the event.

Ted Price, the President of the Messing Committee rose from his chair, next to the Regimental Sergeant Major at the head of the table. Ralph sat on the RSM's right, the place of honour.

'Mister Vice, the Loyal Toast', commanded the PMC. Tradition dictated that the most junior mess member became

JAMES RHYS ROBERTS

Mister Vice, tonight this task fell on the shoulders of newly promoted Fred Tope, who sat at the far end of the table.

Fred, a clerk from the orderly room, just managed to rise from his seat, he was well and truly pissed.

'Gentlemen, please be upstanding for the Loyal Toast' suggested Fred, unsteady on his feet.
Everyone stood, chairs rattled, jokes were ended, the room became silent.

'Gentlemen, Her Majesty the Queen,' almost slurred Fred.

'The Queen!' was the loud reply of everyone in the room.
This was followed by virtually every man in the room washing back the small glass of Taylor's port that each had been served. Everyone sat back down and a burst of laughter rang out as Mr Vice landed flat on his backside; his seat had been removed during the toast.

'Rap, Rap, Rap!' again the gavel was struck.
Ted stood again.

'Gentlemen, the Regimental Sergeant-Major'.

The RSM rose to his feet, not a big man as perhaps an outsider may imagine, but a thin-faced, dark, wiry character. Kenny Harding had been Ralph's Platoon Sergeant when he had joined C Company all those eighteen years ago. Although friendly, approachable and respected by all, he was feared by the junior ranks and admired by his mess members. He had a reputation for being straight down the line. Never one to suffer fools lightly he would rip into both friends and enemies alike, should they not come up to the required standard. Smart as paint in his immaculate mess dress, he would probably drink all and sundry under the table but at the end of the night he would still be immaculate. He never let his guard down. His chest sported the MBE, Northern Ireland Medal (GSM), and like most people

SCAPEGOAT

in the room the Long Service and Good Conduct Medal (LS&GC), known in the Mess as the Long Slogging and Good Climbing Medal.

'Gentlemen', the RSM began.

'We all know why we are assembled here tonight, but firstly I will take this opportunity to update you all on the plans for the Battalion for the next year or so. As you are all aware there are rumblings in certain quarters that the Parachute Brigade are not contributing to the Armies efforts in the likes of Bosnia and Kosova'.

The room was full of muttering and small groups grumbling to each other.

'The Commanding Officer has asked me to pass on that he cannot promise that this Battalion will not be dicked into joining the UN force, but it is being resisted at the highest level. It is also interesting to note that the moaning Crap-hat General's were not so forthcoming when you had all chalked up nine tours of Northern Ireland in the early seventies. We didn't bleat for their help!' The RSM almost shouted.

The room exploded, glasses were banged on the tables, the more reserved members voiced, 'Hear, hear!'

'After all, we have sent our best cunning linguist!' He added making reference to one of the regiment's captains who had just gone absent to live with a local translator in one of the eastern countries. The Mess member's applause changed into laughter. The RSM raised his left hand slowly, and the audience became more controlled.

'Right, let's get down to the more important business. Tonight we are gathered to say goodbye, and to show our appreciation to our friend and colleague, Ralph Ellis. Ralph, as you all know, has decided to no longer take the Queens shilling but to cut and run. Who can blame him? I'm sure no one will condemn you for taking redundancy, Ralph.'

The RSM paused and took a sip from his port glass.

'All of you know Ralph, but few of you know that I owe my life to him and his mate Andy Woods. But that's another story with which I won't bore you, suffice it to say I am very grateful,' was that a tear in the RSM's eye? Surely not!

The room was now icily silent, all present paying full attention.

'This regiment will be poorer for the loss of colour sergeant Ellis and his good lady, Margaret. Both have supported the Mess and it's members throughout the good times, and the bad. I can honestly say that I have not met a more professional soldier throughout my career. It just leaves me to wish both Ralph and Margaret all the best for the future. And to ask Ralph to be gentle with me when he catches me speeding through Mid Yorkshire. Gentlemen! The Armies loss is he Police's gain, I give you Ralph Ellis!' The RSM raised his glass in toast; everyone stood up and followed suit.

'Ralph Ellis!' Everyone repeated, and followed this by swilling back the port.

Instead of sitting down everyone stood applauding, it was a chance for the assembled group to show Ralph their appreciation and express their friendship and feelings for him. Ralph was gobsmacked, he had always stood in the shadows only coming to the fore when needed, then quickly returning to the wings. He had always gone out of his way to help others, but this came naturally to him, he had not expected any thanks. Ralph had not realised he was so popular, he had not realised the strength of feeling towards him. This made leaving even more difficult, he felt like running out screaming.

SCAPEGOAT

'Speech, speech!' Everyone was shouting.

Ralph rose to his feet in a slow and deliberate manner and a hush descended over the room. Ralph paused looking at all the faces, some he knew well, some hardly at all. Many he had shared fear with, some he had shared women with, all he had shared comradeship with. He would miss this, civilians never experienced this unique bond of friendship. This was feeling and mutual respect of the rawest kind, it could almost be touched. A throat clearing cough and Ralph began.

'Regimental Sergeant Major, PMC, Mess Members and Mr Vice when he gets up off his arse'.

A rumble of laughter rippled through the room, Ralph continued.

'Firstly I would like to thank you all for doing me the honour of dining me out this evening. This is an evening I've dreaded the arrival of for many years. I have often sat in a trench or sangar attempting to design this speech, I only wish I'd written a few notes so I'd have a clue what to say now. It's strange you know, you spend all your service wishing for this day and when it arrives you don't want to go'. Ralph's voice had lowered; he was almost talking to himself. He seemed to suddenly realise this and coughed again, falsely.

'Gentlemen!' His voice much louder now.

'On behalf of my wife, Margaret, I would like to thankyou for the years of friendship, she would have liked to have been here herself, but I wouldn't let her!' More laughter.

'On a more serious note, the last one I promise, I will miss you all and I will miss this regiment'. Ralph's voice was faltering again.

'Gentlemen!' Ralph announced, again almost shouting.

'The Regiment!'

Again everyone came to their feet, repeated the toast loudly and washed back more port, and sat back down. There was a sudden flurry of activity as waiters entered the room bearing trays of coffee, and additional decanters of port. Ralph quickly hijacked a full decanter for his personal enjoyment, turned and replenished the RSM's glass without bothering to offer, then sat back and surveyed the gathering. He rarely smoked but now leant forward and helped himself to one of the King Edward's from the silver box in front of him. The RSM and PMC were engrossed in Mess rubbish, Ralph, for the moment, was on an island of his own. In a deliberate manner he lit the cigar, and rocked back in his seat. He looked about, as many memories raced through his mind. He had dined here many times, often being in a far worse state than he was at this moment, often with his wife Margaret. Before getting married he had lived upstairs in the Mess for several years, those were good years, carefree years. No responsibilities except getting up in the morning, often waking in need of an introduction to the young lady lying next to him. Then he met Margaret.

She had been the sister of a fellow Senior NCO, attending the wedding of a sister to one of the lads. Ralph had been invited to make up the numbers, it had been one of the best nights of sex he had ever had. He had been introduced to this quiet, almost shy, dark haired woman with a broad Welsh accent. From the first time she had spoken to him, he was in love. She had just recovered from a long-term courtship with a farmer's lad back in Wales, it had been like opening the fridge door and being confronted with a raging fire. They had woken in Ralph's bunk late the following morning, Margaret had been profoundly embarrassed, but they had merged into a continuation of the night's lovemaking. Ralph was besotted.

Ralph leant back in his seat and continued surveying the

SCAPEGOAT

surroundings. He had some good memories of those simple days, no mortgage, no council tax, just work and play. To play hard was the only way when any social life had to be crammed between tours of duty in Ulster. Tours that created friendships, memories, experience and often death. When the troops descended on Aldershot town it was like a flight of mayflies with twenty-four hours to cram in all that life could offer before the return to night patrolling and constant fear that was Ulster.

Again Ralph replenished the RSM's port glass, both men were already on their second glass from the new decanter. A cigar lit, Ralph leaned back in his seat and continues to take in the room. The newer paintings on the walls depicted various members of the Unit carrying out one or another famous act of bravery. One massed produced print was from his mate Andy, presented to the Mess following the siege of the Iranian Embassy. 'The most crowded balcony in the world' as it was known. Although the picture showed only four men from the Regiment, Ralph himself had met at least twenty from Hereford who professed to have been on the balcony.

"I can't imagine you as a copper Ralph, you'll have to watch yourself mate', advised the RSM.

'I'll be all right those criminals won't know what hit them', Ralph replied.

'That's what I'm on about, you won't be able to go round cracking skulls you know, everyone is your enemy in that job - you be careful', The RSM looked Ralph straight in the eye as he spoke.

'I know', was the almost solemn reply.

'And Ralph, I know I've never dwelt on the matter but I will never, ever forget that day in Belfast', the RSM's voice lowered to almost a whisper, he leant nearer to Ralph.

'My wife and children appreciate what you and your mate Andy did that day, my wife told me to say – thankyou'.
Ralph thought he could see a tear in the corner of the RSM's eye, the port or the smoke he thought to himself.

'Piss off you sentimental old twat!' Ralph said smiling, attempting to make light of the matter.

—-oooOOOooo—-

The night air was November sharp, a full moon reflected off the grey slate roof tiles of the Old Park Road. This was Belfast at it's best, the senses on edge, anticipation on every corner. He heard the shot ring out, somewhere from the Ballies. He saw Andy sprint from the shadows and start to drag Kenny from the centre of the road where he had fallen, another shot. Got you, you bastard amateur, he had seen the muzzle of the Remington Woodmaster rifle protruding from the window. Sighting, two quick shots, double tap, from his SLR and Ralph watched as the sniper spun through the window and lay bleeding on the ledge. His AK47 fell clattering to the pavement below. The Irish ballad drifting on the still air;

'And did they believe when they answered the call,
did they really believe that this war would end wars.
But besides all the suffering, the glory, the pain,
the killing and dying was all done in vain.
Cause young Willie McBride it's all happened again,
again and again and again and again.
Did they..................................'

SCAPEGOAT

A blinding light hit Ralph in the eyes, the music stopped abruptly, he looked up from the sofa.

'Shit woman, I was listening to that, turn it back on'.

'Come on Ralph, get to bed the removals arrive in five hours,' His wife, Margaret rubbed her eyes as she spoke. She walked over to her drunken husband and offered him a hand up. He accepted the offer and she pulled him to his feet, the same routine as usual. She was just content to have him home, not laid in some gutter or between some tarts legs. Margaret Ellis was a realist, she had her man, for better or for worse - more often the latter. She liked the Army life, just as she would start to lose her patience with Ralph's drinking and gambling the Army would whip him away somewhere for six month's or so. It was great. Leaving the Army was Ralph's big plan, she had not been consulted on the matter, and she was frightened. I will have to leave in a few years anyway, he would try and persuade her; better to go now and get a bigger handout. Tomorrow, or later today to be more accurate, she and the children and all her earthly belongings would be packed up and carted to the north of England, a new house, new people, and possibly a new Ralph. She had only been to mid Yorkshire once, to choose the house. They had agreed to buy the first one they saw, typical of Ralph, some businessman. All she could remember about the place was the bleak, grey landscape. The closed factories in ruins and the miserable unfriendly faces of the unknown people.

Not at all like her native Wales, the green hills, faces she had grown up with, and places she loved. Ralph had always promised they would return there, one day. He had attempted to join a few Welsh Police forces, but he was English. Ralph reckoned they didn't like the Bastard Race because they could play

JAMES RHYS ROBERTS

rugby. But deep down rejection had got to Ralph he had never failed at anything, yet another new experience he had to get used to. Ralph attempted to reassure her by insisting they would 'one day' return to 'God's Country' as she called her homeland.

CHAPTER THREE

The first peat fires of the autumn sent wisps of light grey smoke from the rows of ageing chimneystacks. Children were called in by their mothers as the night crept in. Belfast was still witnessing the latest uncanny period of peace. This period of cease-fire had gone on for many months, a change of British government had added impetuous to the ongoing talks. The Catholic Ardoyne had a strange atmosphere about it, everyone knew it would take just a wrong word to rekindle the flames of conflict. The mothers calling in their children appreciated every passing day of peace. Most had lost relatives in 'the troubles', many had lost husbands and children. For some the 'lull in the battle', as they called it, was driving them up the wall. The 'Rah', as the IRA was known locally, had recently stopped the weekly payments to its volunteers, now they were fully dependent on the brew. Relying totally on the British Welfare System got to them, they were fiercely proud and felt let down by their leaders. The inactivity made it worse, no more hijackings, no more armed robberies in the name of the cause. No more bombing, shooting or kneecapping. For many this was pure excruciating boredom, and looming poverty.

The red Mercedes cruised slowly up the Crumlin Road, turned right and parked outside the Republican Club. An elderly man leaning against the wall of the building turned and banged out the contents of his pipe on the nearby lamppost. This was the all clear signal, no peelers about, no covert Army observation posts in the derelict houses facing the club. The man in the backseat of the Mercedes quickly got out and almost ran into the club. Once inside he turned right and pushed through a door marked Private, not left which led to the bar area from which the noise and music came flooding. Inside the door a huge man with a full dark beard stepped back to allow the newcomer clear passage.

'How are you Pat?', enquired the beard.

'Fine. Yourself?', came the reply.

'Not so bad'. The beard was not looking at Pat as he spoke but through him, covering the outside door his right hand firmly clenched on the revolver in his shoulder holster under his jacket.

Patrick turned immediately left and took the stairs in front of him two at a time. At the top of the stairs stood another man, again with a hand inside jacket. This time no words were spoken, the man just nodded his head, Patrick gave a return wink at the same time landing a false punch on the arm of the man as he passed. This brought a smile to the man. Turning right along a small landing Patrick opened a door and entered a smoke filled room. The room was dark with no windows, a single electric bulb dangled from a flex in the centre of the room. Sitting around a small table are two men. One, a tidily dressed fresh faced individual stood up and threw his hand out to welcome Patrick. Patrick took the hand and shook it with enthusi-

SCAPEGOAT

asm. The other, red headed, almost scruffily clad, lolled back on his chair, a glass of whisky in his hand. Patrick looked at him.

'Seamus.'

'Patrick', the man half-heartedly replied.

'And Sean, yourself?' Patrick addressed the younger man.

'Fine, fine Patrick'.

On the table stood a half-empty bottle of fine Irish whisky, two glasses and an overflowing ashtray. With his brushed back, neatly clipped greying hair and his long dark pure wool overcoat, Patrick didn't seem to suit his surroundings. He looked more as if he had just left his City office and taken a wrong turning.

'I see you found the bottle then Seamus', Patrick spoke as he leant forward and filled both his and Sean's glasses.

'We have been kept waiting you know, you said nine o'clock', Seamus said as he rocked forward, grabbed the bottle and emptied the remains into his glass.

'Aye, I know. The man in Dublin had a lot to say. A lot', Patrick said calmly, but meaningfully, as he placed his whisky glass onto the table. Patrick continued.

'Right, you two listen, and listen fucking good, yer hear, especially you Seamus; I want no more fuckup's', Patrick looked directly at Seamus as he spoke.

'The man is not fucking happy, the volunteers are not fucking happy, and I'm definitely not fucking happy, that's for sure. What started as yet another cease-fire, just a wee rest for the boys to get their shit together, has turned into a serious threat to business. People are getting used to the peace, even our so called leaders are in the talks. The women like the peace so they say, the women would like the troubles to end for good, so they say. Women are running the fucking show, it's no good!' Patrick picked his glass up and washed back the remaining golden liquid.

'It's got to bloody well end, and that's why we're here tonight,' Patrick stood up from his chair and slowly wondered around the small room.

'I told you that at the fucking outset', muttered Seamus into his glass.

'Dublin has decided that more radical measures are needed, I could not agree more'.

Patrick still slowly walking around the room turned to face the men and lowered his voice.

'We cannot afford the bloody peace, our rackets are drying up with the peelers now having time to hit our dealers, our protection boy's are getting laughed at, it's got to finish'.

'Easier said than done', Sean spoke for the first time, 'the people are getting used to the peace now, they'll turn against whoever spoils their quiet nights'. Sean took the first and smallest sip from his glass.

'Yes Sean me boy, but we're not going to be the nasty bastards who restart the war, not this time', Patrick had a sinister smile across his face.

'We've been talking to a friend of ours, a Protestant friend of ours. You didn't know we had such friends, did you?' Neither man replied.

'Well, we have and he's a very senior man, is our friend. And it's in his interest as much as ours to have the troubles back, everyone is losing money, including our friend'.

Seamus rocked violently for in his chair, slammed the now empty glass on the table and stood up abruptly.

'You mean after all the fucking goings on of the last twenty years you expect us to work with the fucking Orange bastards! You must be taking the fucking piss!' Seamus was almost shout-

ing now as he now started pacing around the room.
Patrick leant forward with straight arms on the back of a chair.

'Wind your bloody neck in you, you know nothing, we've been working with the 'Orange Bastards' as you call them for years now, who do you think organises all the speed and ecstasy from Holland?' Patrick took a quick, agitated swig from the whisky glass. His patience with Seamus always wore thin quickly, but the man had his uses.

'Who do you think produces all the porn, Seamus my boy you know absolutely fucking nothing!'

'Fuck, fuck, fuck!' Seamus spat the words through his clenched teeth as he paced around the room. Sean remained calm and said nothing, a totally different animal to Seamus, Sean had suspected such dealings for years.

'And what about the mainland. We wouldn't survive without our Prot contacts - and they couldn't survive without us.' As Patrick spoke he walked over to Seamus, and put his arm around his shoulders.

'If you don't like it you can always get out you know, but even in peacetime there's only one way out, you should know that Seamus, and it will do you good to remember that me boy'. Patrick spoke quietly, but firmly. Seamus looked at him, said nothing and sat down like an obedient spaniel.

'Now that's all over let's get down to detail,' Patrick took a chair turned it backwards and sat at the table with his arms across the top of chair.

'Our Orange friend has ambitions, his top man won't live forever, in fact if rumours are to be believed he's not got many years left to scream down from the pulpit. Our man is the next in line so we have one major obstacle. But this obstacle could prove useful, our man reckons that should anything untoward happen to this individual the Prots would start the troubles overnight, without our help.'

'Yes, but surely we will still get the blame.' Sean added.

'Exactly, Sean me boy, that's our little problem. We need someone to carry out our dirty work, someone to shift the blame elsewhere, a scapegoat that's what we need. Whoever it is should not bring the blame back to our fucking doorstep.' Patrick paused and looked at the two men. He continued.

'It's not an easy one, put your minds to it, keep it tight. Take your time it's got to work well so think it out before you waste everyone's time. Right?' Patrick did not wait for a reply, he stood abruptly and headed for the door. As he opened it he turned back towards the two left at the table.

'I'll get in touch when I need to see you again. Remember, this one stays with us three.'

Patrick left the room and quickly passed the two doormen without comment, he paused in the outside doorway waiting for the Mercedes to arrive, which it did in seconds. As he got into the back of the car he turned towards the old man with the pipe and gave him the slightest of winks. The old man made no acknowledgement.

'Your Da's looking well.' said the driver, as he slid the Merc into gear.

'Aye, remind me to send him some baccy for that pipe of his will yer.'

The Mercedes moved away from the City, into the night. It would take them half an hour to get to Patrick's house on the banks of Lough Neagh. His four acres, horses and respectability. Half an hour, but a million miles from where he had come from.

Back in the Club Seamus and Sean had made their way down-

SCAPEGOAT

stairs from the small room and were stood in the bar. The evening was going well, the regular band was banging out their repertoire of Republican songs fluctuating between tearful ballads and thumping war cries. The locals joining in with the choruses believing the songs portrayed the whole situation of the cause, freedom, the fighting and the dying. Very few of them were aware of the true motivation behind 'the troubles', the corruption and greed on both sides of the political coin. Seamus turned to Sean and leant over to make himself heard over the chorus of The Men Behind the Wire.

'What do you make of that shite up them stairs?'

'Let's talk later, not here, you were told,' almost whispered Sean in response.

'Fuck him he's just a bastard message boy, you tell me if there's so much to lose where's all the fucking money going now, eh?'

'Keep it down!' Sean said raising his voice as if to add meaning.

'I'll tell you where it's fucking going will I, in the likes of Patrick Fucking Kelly's pocket, that where. Him and his big house, horses and fucking whore!' Seamus let rip a loud belch as he finished his speech. Sean looked at him in disgust and again whispered.

'The way your going you're going to end up with a hole behind your ear, and it won't be for putting a fucking earring in I can tell you.'

'Excuse me lads!' shouted the old man with the pipe who had been waiting behind them to get served.

'No problem,' replied Seamus as he stood back to make way.

JAMES RHYS ROBERTS

—-oooOOOooo—-

Seamus stood swaying in an alcoholic haze looking around the Club. He was trying to think out all that had been said that night, the two or so pints of whisky he had taken wasn't helping the thought process. He thought of all the mates he had lost over the years, for what? He looked at all the Republican regalia on the walls, hand stitched in the Maze. The perfect replica of the Armorlite rifle carved in the early days in Armagh jail. The rows of embroidered pictures of the 'Martyrs'. A smile came to his face as he remembered that several years before some woman had stuck up a poster for the Slimming Club right under a picture of one of the hunger strikers. The woman had taken a beating from her husband for the slight oversight. The smile remained as he washed back yet another glass of Bush.

The smile grew as he looked across the room, there sitting next to her elderly mother was none other than Katey McQuire, the touts wife. Seamus had always fancied a bit of her even from back at school. She had kept her slim figure over the years, her red hair falling naturally almost to her waist. Seamus could clearly make out the outline of her full, firm breasts, having two children had not seen her go to seed. Her husband, Liam, had been the best Quartermaster the Belfast Brigade had ever had. Or so they thought until things started going wrong, three times on the trot the Army had ambushed and killed the volunteer's moments after Liam had delivered the weapons. Once too often to be a coincidence Patrick Kelly had thought, especially as one of the victims of the Special Air Services latest success had been his very own brother. Two days later in the early hours of the morning Katey had been woken by loud bangs on the front door of their terraced house.

SCAPEGOAT

She had looked from the bedroom window to see two men dressed in black, with black balaclavas on and carrying handguns. They had shouted up for her to get her man out of bed. She had roused Liam from his drunken slumbers thinking they needed him for a job. Liam had gone down to them with a towel wrapped around his waist. They had bundled him into the waiting car and driven off at speed.

Seamus could remember it well he had pushed the barrel of the Smith and Wesson revolver hard into the back of Liam's neck all the way to the border. He could recall the days of beatings that Liam had received, the pliers and the cigarette ends, before Liam inevitably confessed when it was suggested his wife might know the answers they wanted. He continued to smile as he remembered the screams from Liam as he was dragged into the farmer's field.

'One thing, one thing please, give my love to Katey', Liam had pleaded as Seamus had put the gun to his head. Seamus had replied

'Don't worry Liam I'll do that for you, I'll surely do that' and had then pulled the trigger.

The old lady got up from her seat and went towards the toilets; Seamus seized his chance and walked across to the table.

'How are you Katey, long time no see?'
Katey looked straight at him and said nothing.

'Come on Touts Wife, speak to a Volunteer when you're spoken to!'
Katey continued the same stare of hatred and slowly spoke.

'I'm no fucking informers wife and you know it Seamus Quigley, my husband lived true to the cause and died true to the cause'.

'Aye, I'm sure you're right.' Seamus sat down opposite her and leant over.

'What are you doing for a man nowadays then, I bet you're missing your Liam in more ways than one, eh?'

In an instance Katey had pulled the table towards her and upwards sending Seamus crashing to the floor. Several empty glasses and a few full one's smashed about him. She bent over and pushed him over with her foot unceremoniously, there was blood running from a glass cut on his forehead.

The band suddenly stopped playing and everyone in the Club went quiet and turned to look over at the source of the commotion.

'Seamus Quigley you and your type should not be allowed to walk this earth, you are nothing but scum!' She screamed
Katey picked up her handbag, took the hand of her mother who had returned to see the mess and both walked quickly towards the exit.

Quigley just lay in the broken glass and mess laughing and shouting.

'I'll give you what you need woman, just you fucking see girl, just you fucking see!'
Sean stood some distance away, but did nothing to assist his disgraced drunken colleague.

—-oooOOOooo—-

'Cor, someone's upset her!' The soldier said quietly as he watched the red head storm from the Club almost dragging the old lady behind her.

'She's cursing like a good 'un'.

'Here they come now Andy.' The SAS man spoke again to his

partner.

'Yeah, both of them, Sean and Seamus.' He continued giving a running commentary as he looked though the lens of the infrared video camera.

'Something's going down, you don't get them two and Kelly together just for a social drink.' Andy said in a whisper to his colleague behind the camera. The additional camera mounted next to them recorded everyone who entered or left the Club.

It had been Andy's idea to occupy the house when they saw the elderly couple depart for Spain for their annual break from the 'strife torn province'. Everyone knew it was a waste of time trying to get an observation post in the derelicts opposite. It had been done too often as the Artillery close observation platoon had found out when they had returned to the derelict for a second time to be welcomed by a length of fishing line attached to a grenade. Crude but effective, as both soldiers would have testified had they survived.

The two SAS men had been in the Province for four months, the tenth time they had been sent across at short notice to carry out a quick 'one off', operation. You can tell when an Officer is lying; his lips move. Andy would always tell his Patrol. Both Andy and Pete were veterans of this type of warfare. Their present location was considered near luxury. It was dry, warm, and even had a toilet. Albeit used with a bin bag draped under the seat to catch their efforts in order to avoid having to flush the loo. (They did not want to give the impression to the neighbours that compo-constipated ghosts haunted the house.)

'Another two hours and we'll be off.' Said Andy under his breath.

Leaving would be a doddle, they had used a screwdriver to

force a kitchen window but caused no damage. When they left all they had to do was pull the door shut, luckily the old couple had not fitted a deadlock. Pity they would have to wait another twelve months before they could use it again, holidays permitting. They started to pack everything and clean the bedroom, which had been home for the last seven days. There would be no hint of their presence. In the past week they had kept their movements to a minimum and any rubbish had been packed as it appeared.

The pickup car was bang on time; much to Andy's annoyance the new Troop Commander was driving. 'Jumped up fucking Rupert' Andy thought to himself as he quietly placed the Bergen's in the boot and pushed it gently shut. Both men jumped into the car, and it sped away, much too fast for Andy's liking.

'Did you hear about the meeting Sir?' Andy said as they turned onto the Crumlin Road.

'What meeting?' replied the Captain.

'Patrick Kelly, Seamus Quigley and Sean Miller. At the Club tonight'.

'Come on Sergeant Woods you see 'meetings' everywhere, it's a Nationalist Club remember, they all drink together.' The mocking tone of the Captains reply added to Andy's annoyance.

'You mean you haven't informed the Branch?' Andy asked aggressively.

'No way, its their Autumn Bash tonight, it's not important. I'll mention it at prayers in the morning.'
The Officer turned the car into the Army camp. They spoke no more.

—-oooOOOooo—-

SCAPEGOAT

'Hello, is that you Brian, its Andy across at the Troop.' Andy said into the phone, 'Just thought I'd let you know we saw Patrick, Seamus and Sean out tonight.'
Andy paused.
'Yeah, at the usual place.' Another longer pause.
'Yeah, I did tell him, four hours ago, but he said it wasn't important he'd let you know in the morning. Andy stood listening, shaking his head, he then replaced the handset and walked over towards the bar to get shit faced.
Andy was sound asleep when the intercom buzzer sounded, he rolled over and looked at the clock; eleven o'clock, 'shit, I only left the bar an hour ago', he thought to himself.
'Yes!' Andy shouted into the intercom above his bed.
'Sgt Woods, Captain Thackray- Smith would appreciate your presence in his office.' Said the Duty Signaller.
'Tell him to fuck off!' Andy shouted.
'You just have,' the Signaller replied.
'Sgt Woods, my office. Now!' The Captain ordered, leaning over the Signaller.
'Yes Sir!' Responded Andy in his most subservient manner.
Andy pulled on his tracksuit on his way to the office complex. Having not slept properly for several days and then having consumed a least a gallon of beer before breakfast he did not feel in the mood for this shit. He knocked on the Captains office door, a voice replied.
'Come in! Shut the door Woods.' Ordered the Captain. Andy turned and pushed the door shut, firmly.
'Listen Woods you have made a complete prat out of me.' Captain Thackray-Smith was trying to hide his temper, but failing.

'Even the Commanding Officer has seen fit to ring me from Hereford and advice me on my shortcomings. To say the least Woods I am not impressed with you going behind my back.'

'Well I did tell you in the car Sir, piss up or no piss up the Branch would want to know immediately if Kelly was involved in anything, but you wouldn't listen.' Andy retorted as he stood hands in track bottoms cupping his 'brains' as his wife called them. He could not for the life of him enter into the spirit of this bollocking.

'Listen Sir.....' Andy started to say.

'No! You listen Sergeant! I intend to command this Regiment, just like my father did, and I will not let a little upstart like you get in my way. So tread very carefully, do you understand?' The Captain was red faced and shaking with temper.

'Yes Sir, but remember, I served under your father in Dhofar and can assure you, you are not fit to lick his boots. He would never have come out with a statement like that. Be careful who you threaten in this Regiment Sir, or one day someone may take you seriously.' Andy spoke calmly, but with sincere meaning. The Captain seemed stunned. Andy turned, opened the door and walked unhurried from the office. As he left the complex he could be heard whistling loudly 'The Ride of the Valkyries".

CHAPTER FOUR

The move to Mid Yorkshire had gone quite smoothly, Margaret had seen to most of the organising, Ralph taking a backseat in the affair, as usual. Shirefield was just as depressing as Margaret remembered, but luckily she hardly had time to think about it as she waded into the task of moving. She wanted everything just right, straight way. She kept telling Ralph to get out of the house as he was getting in the way. The children started attending the school just around the corner the day after they arrived, so they were out from under their mother's feet. Both children had come home from school crying each afternoon, some 'big boys' had hit Simon, who had just celebrated his tenth birthday. Charlotte just wasn't happy, so she had joined in the crying. Their new house was on the outskirts of the empty decaying shell of what used to be a prosperous industrial city. Various immigrant communities, drug pushers and thieves had filled the industrial void. The first significant job Margaret found for her husband was the fitting of the burglar alarm. They had noticed straight away that theirs was the only house without one. The feeling of being threatened in their own home was new to them and made them feel uncomfortable.

Ralph was bored shitless. When he was told to get out of the house 'and do something useful' he would either go for a long run over the grey hills of the open cast mine opposite, or just sit and read yet another novel. On the few occasions he ventured into the local pub he felt like an alien. The miserable customers would turn to look at him with suspicion, and say nothing. On about his fourth lunchtime visit one chap did start to talk.

'Ah, ex Para eh, my Dad was a Para in the war.' said the man as he rolled a cigarette.

'Yes, eighteen years, just made redundant, volunteered like.' Added Ralph.

'What you going to be doing up here then, ain't no work up here you know.'

'Going to be a copper, I start training week after next.'

Ralph took a mouthful of beer. As he lowered his glass he saw the man walk away into the other bar, mumbling something Ralph couldn't make out.

'I wouldn't be shouting about becoming a copper around here mate, to most locals the miners strike was last week, they've got long memories.'

The advice had come from the barman who was putting glasses under the bar in front of Ralph, he hadn't bothered to look up as he spoke. Ralph took the man's advice, supped up and left the pub. From that day Ralph would walk to the pub which was about two miles away, and when asked what he did he would proudly state he was an 'ex Para', but was now unemployed.

At last the day arrived when Ralph could go off to the Police Training Centre and busy himself. The Army had sent the redundancy payment to his bank, after all the new furniture and

SCAPEGOAT

electrical goods were paid for there was still over fifteen grand left. He had never been so well off. He also bought himself a decent second hand car, as they now needed two. All in all he felt quite full of himself as he sped up the motorway. He had spent a few days at his own force training centre and had been issued with his new uniform and silly hat. His pride and joy was the carbon steel telescopic baton they had given him. Collapsed, this item looked inoffensive, but extended Ralph could tell it was capable of breaking bones. He settled into training quickly having spent most of his adult life in one Army camp or another this was a piece of piss. He found the almost total lack of discipline disconcerting. His stumbling block was going to be the political correctness that was required. He knew to mention a racially derogative remark would be the end of his police career before it began, but constantly referring to the senior ranks as 'supervisors' just didn't seem right to Ralph. Almost half the recruits were female and sexist remarks were frowned on. Ralph had 'A Levels' in sexist remarks, at the start of one discussion on this subject Ralph asked, 'How many black men does it take to clean a toilet?'
No one replied.

'None, its a woman's job!' Ralph had laughingly said.
No one had joined in his mirth, especially not the Instructor. Later that day he had been called to the Chief Instructors Office to explain his remarks. Ralph, thinking on his feet, had made an attempt to explain it away as an effort to highlight other people's prejudices. The Chief Instructor, a greying 'old school' Chief Inspector had not believed him. From then on Ralph watched every word he said.

The highlight had been the riot training; this was the nearest subject to his Army life. Ralph enjoyed it all, the running about, the drills and the violence. It also highlighted the weakness of some of the women, one of whome was incapable of making it all the way to the drill square carrying her riot shield. At least she didn't belong to his force so she wouldn't be coming to rescue him if he was in trouble.

Ralph managed to complete the first ten weeks of training before returning to Shirefield to do some 'on the streets' tuition. His tutor was a young female and although this was even more alien to his experience he identified immediately that she was a dedicated and efficient police officer. He knew instinctively that he would get on with her, although he had to watch his one off quips, but all in all, he was impressed with the methods of his newfound friend and mentor. She spent every meal break in the gym, he tended to play snooker or eat a steaming curry from the takeaway across the road. At last he started to enjoy his new job, even the long foot patrols in the rain.

At home Margaret was not a happy woman. It was obvious that the word had got around the estate that Ralph was a 'pig' .The neighbours who had initially talked on their arrival now totally ignored them. The children were still getting more and more grief at school and came home most afternoons crying. At every opportunity Margaret took the children to see their granny in Wales. Each weekend she would threaten not to return, leaving it till late Sunday night to make the journey back to the place she most hated. One such Sunday evening she had phoned to say that her mother was ill and she was going to stay the week to look after her. She had also arranged with the local village school for the children to attend just for that week. Ralph, blinded by being totally absorbed by his new career, just agreed and went to the pub. Ralph was glad of the

SCAPEGOAT

rest from the constant arguing, he was on day shift but managed to get into the pub every night. The following weekend his wife returned without the children much to Ralph's surprise. Margaret explained that it was only three weeks to half term so it seemed a better idea to leave the children in school, she did not mention that they had flatly refused to return to their new home.

They still did nothing but argue with Ralph always storming out to the pub. Ralph had never been an aggressive man at home. He had never in all his years of marriage even thought of striking his wife. After yet another argument he had gone to the pub and taken his fill. He had staggered home, more pissed than usual. In the pub he had been invited into a 'friendly' game of cards.

'Back to the gambling again are you?' She had shouted at him as he sat in his drunken stupor in the new armchair.

'It was only pennies, honestly love.' He managed to slur before momentarily falling asleep, his dinner on the table in front of him.

'Why do I bloody well bother?' Margaret muttered to herself as she picked up the hot plate and scrapped the meal into the bin in the kitchen. As she turned to put the plate into the sink she heard Ralph stir.

'Where's my fucking dinner gone?' He shouted as he staggered into the kitchen to see the empty plate in his wife's hand. Ralph lost it, and moved quickly towards Margaret raising the back of his hand. His foot caught the carpet and he fell forward, knocking her sideways before falling to the floor with a thud. As she fell her head hit the corner of the cupboard and blood ran freely from the resulting wound. Ralph lay in a heap where he fell and began to snore gently.

37

JAMES RHYS ROBERTS

Without a second thought Margaret rose and put a towel to the cut on her head. She started packing. Within minutes two large bags were packed with necessities for herself and the children, and she didn't even bother to look back as she drove away from the house towards the motorway and Wales. Ralph remained on the floor, snoring.

The continuous ringing of the telephone eventually woke Ralph. He looked at his watch, shit! Severn o' clock and he was supposed to be on shift at six. The civilian switchboard operator at the police station was very abrupt. His instinctive excuse of having flu had been quite convincing and the alcohol-induced gravel in his voice had added substance to his excuse. He would take a couple of days off just to add more substance. He made himself a cup of coffee and turned on the television. Yes, the gorilla had mugged him, he thought to himself.

'Pinched all me money and shit in me mouth.' He muttered to himself as he crashed out on the sofa.

As he sipped his coffee he started to mull over the previous nights happenings. He could remember getting involved in the card game, he recalled the two gypsy types joining the game and immediately upping the stakes. By then he had been well into the staggering stage, bouncing off the walls as he went to the loo for a much-needed leak. When he returned to the table he hadn't registered that all the regular players had become spectators. He continued the game with the two rough looking characters. The hundred quid he had in his wallet lasted about twenty minutes. He could remember signing several IOU's which he was to pay off today. How he would have managed that if he had managed to get up for work, he didn't know, but now he would get it all sorted out at lunchtime, he could do without enemies the like of the two gypsies. Then in a blinding flash he remembered the argument with Margaret, he jumped to his feet and almost ran upstairs. The bedrooms were empty, drawers were ajar with items of clothing hanging to the floor. No Margaret, no children. All at once his life seemed empty. He slumped onto the bed, head in hands and tears in eyes.

'Margaret, come back, I love you.' He pleaded with the wedding photograph on the cabinet next to the bed.

—--oooOOOooo—--

A couple of hours later Ralph awoke. He was not happy, but he made a mental plan of action before fully rising. He would phone Margaret at her mothers before anything else. A thousand sorry's would do the trick, he thought confidently. Then he would get to the pub and sort out the bill with the two gypsies, he didn't want them as enemies, that was for sure. He rolled over and picked up the phone.

'She does not want to talk to you, don't you understand!' Margaret's mother said sternly

'But she's got to, I'm her bloody husband, it was only a stupid argument.'

'Well you can't talk to her, she's not here,' the mother in law continued obviously enjoying her task,

'And she hasn't been here either, she's found a better place to live and a better man to live with!'

'What the fuck do you mean, you cow, you never did like me!' Ralph couldn't believe what he was hearing. His whole life started flashing in front of him, his wife, his children and his home all gone. He sat stunned, the phone still in his hand he just looked blankly out of the window at the bleak, sorry landscape.

'So who is this bloke then?' Ralph's voice had become almost weak.

'What, so you can come down and batter him, you just leave them alone boyo. Gareth will look after the kids better than you ever did.' She replied with more than a little hatred in her tone. It was true she had never forgiven him for taking her daughter away from the village.

'We'll see what kind of man Gareth is when I get my fucking hands on him, won't we!'

Ralph spat the words out as he slammed down the phone, a fragment of plastic was sent flying across the bedroom as a result.

Anger took over from love as he stormed through the house kicking any furniture that had the audacity to get in his way. He tried to persuade himself that he didn't care and that there was a certain attraction to being a single man in this city. But this was a sham, deep down he was hurting like he had never hurt before. His whole life seemed to have gone rotten since leaving the Army and moving to this shit tip of a place. He swigged back the remains of a pint of milk from the fridge, threw a jacket on and made for the door. He hadn't washed or shaved, he had slept in his clothes. Now, he just needed a drink. He suddenly remembered the gypsies and grabbed his cheque-book from the kitchen table as he left.

The larger of the two gypsies stood as Ralph walked into the bar. The man was about six foot four with a thick matted beard covering most of his face. His hands were like coal shovels, with dirt engrained in every pore. Ralph had noticed several deep red scars on this creatures hands as he had dealt the cards the

SCAPEGOAT

day before. Not a man to tangle with, that was for sure.

'We didn't think you were going to show, just about to pay you a visit we were.' The man had a false friendly smile across his face.

'No, I'm here, I always pay my debts.' Ralph said loud enough for the other gypsy to hear as he turned to the bar and ordered a beer.

'Mine's a bitter, so's me mates.' The big man stated as he placed his empty glass on the bar next to Ralph.

Once served both men joined the man at the table.

'Your health.' Said the man who was slightly shorter than his colleague, but thicker set. This man was obviously the brains of the outfit, he seemed to pause and think before he embarked upon a sentence. Ralph found this most unnerving. The man swallowed half the pint in two gulps before placing the glass on the table.

'Right, business before pleasure.' He said as he reached into his pocket and pulled out several small, crumpled sheets of paper. He then went on to spread each piece of paper out flat on the table.

'Four hundred and twenty quid, I make it, count them if you want.'
Ralph went pale.

'What do you mean, we only played for an hour or, you must be joking.'
Ralph reached across the table and picked up one of the pieces of paper. There written as plain as day, IOU, One Hundred and Ten Pounds, signed Ralph. He reached for another.

'Wait a bloody minute, that's not my signature.' Ralph knew he was being ripped off.
The big man leant forward, empty pint glass in hand.

41

JAMES RHYS ROBERTS

'Are you calling my brother a liar?' The man almost whispered, pointing the glass at Ralph. Ralph knew when to advance and when to retreat.

'No, not at all, after all I was very drunk yesterday.' Ralph pulled the chequebook from his inside pocket, a pen was thrown onto the table. The cheque signed, and handed over both gypsies stood abruptly and turned to leave. The brains of the two turned.

'And you just pray this cheque doesn't turn into a bloody basket ball or we'll be paying you a visit.'

Ralph finished his beer, stood up and walked over to the bar. He ordered another and stood in deep thought, the beer making him feel almost human again. Well it could have been worse, he thought to himself, he had money to spare at the moment, no injuries, he would put the whole incident down to experience. What about the wife? Ralph couldn't be bothered to tackle that one at the moment. He was too upset and it was too complicated. After all, he said to himself, he had known deep down inside that something was wrong, they hadn't made love for several weeks. Shift work meant you had to grab the opportunity whenever it arose, Margaret had always found one excuse or another. That was when she was at home, not away in Wales getting pumped by her darling Gareth. Ralph was confident that she would be back, this aspect made Ralph's mind race. He would try to turn the sorry circumstances into an expedition. There was many a foresty cleft he wanted to explore before his wife decided to return. Well at least that cheered him up for the moment.

He stayed in the pub for another half a dozen pints then made his way home through the rain. On the way he picked up

SCAPEGOAT

pie and chips, there would be no dinner on the table tonight. He watched the television for an hour and then fell asleep on the sofa, having resisted the temptation to phone Wales. He did not want to be late for work again, he was a professional, he reminded himself. Afterall he did enjoy his new job, especially when he was out on his own not having to defer to some of the strange ways of his colleagues. He had no time for most of the women in the job. 'Why do we have Policewomen? One of the blokes had quipped, 'because police dogs can't answer the telephone', had been the reply. In the main Ralph agreed with this philosophy, although some of the girls outshone several of the blokes. Next week he would have to return to the Training School, the final session of mind mapping. He would have to watch every word he said, he knew the Instructors would be keeping an eye on him this time.

—-oooOOOooo—-

'Will tea be fine, I've run out of coffee?' Katey asked her visitor.

'Aye, that'll be good.' Sean replied.

It had been a few days since the incident at the club and she hoped it had become history. Sean had been a close friend of Liam and did not believe he had been a tout, not Liam, he had been one of the first to join the Provos along with Sean and a few others. Sean had continued to visit Katey and the children, even though many would be quick to throw scorn on his association with a Touts wife. He always made sure she was all right, always gave the kids a few quid. This always resulted in theatrical refusal by Katey who was embarrassed by the charity. But he always insisted, he knew times were hard for her now. They were like sister and brother. They had grown up on the same terraced row, there was never any suggestion of Sean 'trying it on', and she felt at ease with him.

'Seamus is still ranting and raving about the other night at the club you know. He's a worm, men like him are a good advert for abortion, his mother should have done the world a favour when she first laid eyes on him'. She said with hatred in her words.

'Well, you had better be careful when he's about. Watch him, he's a dangerous bastard that one.'

Kate turned to pour the tea, smiling as if the likes of Seamus Quigley weren't worth worrying about, but inside she was petrified of the man. Every night she expected him to come knocking on her door to take his revenge.

'Don't you worry yourself Sean, I'll be staying well out the way of the likes of Mr Quigley. My sister is always trying to get us to join her in Canada, but I think I would miss me Ma too much'

Katey kept an immaculately clean house. Although a small two up, two down terrace, it was warm and welcoming. Sean enjoyed his visits, he liked to escape from the small flat he had to share with Seamus on the Falls Road. Escape from the dingy, dark, dank smell of that evil man. Everything about him stank, his body, his clothes, his stale whisky, cigarettes, and sweat. But the main thing that stunk about Seamus, was Seamus. He was everything that was wrong with the world, he had no respect for people, their property or their lives. Seamus could shoot the kneecaps of a youth as if he were poking a fire, it meant that much to him. Sean had seen the sinister smile on his

SCAPEGOAT

face the night he topped Liam. Sean had felt so helpless, but this was not to be discussed with Katey, never, ever.

'The girls still a handful then?' Sean changed the subject.

'Oh, they're both good girls. Mary is going to marry Robson Green, and Shirley is marrying all of Boyzone, at once!' Katey was smiling now.

A repetitious purring sound came from Sean's inside pocket, he reached inside and pulled out the offending mobile telephone.

'Yes, I know, I won't be late I'm on my way now.' Sean looked embarrassed as he spoke into the contraption.

'Sorry, duty calls.' He leant over to Katey and landed a peck on her cheek, at the same time pressing a roll of notes into her hand.

'No, I don't need that, you take it back now!' She demanded, half-heartedly.

'Now come on Katey, you know you need it, buy the girls a new dress or something.'

'You're a good man Sean. Liam knew how to pick his friends that's for sure.'

CHAPTER FIVE

Sean was cursing as he guided the Toyota onto the motorway out of Belfast. Quigley was always chasing Sean about, never happy when he couldn't see him, always thought he was missing out on something. If Seamus had known that he had been drinking tea with the tout's wife when he rang, he would have been more than a little jealous. He turned the car stereo up loud as he accelerated north towards Larne. The ferry was not due to berth for an hour, so there was no real rush, but Sean always liked to arrive in the area early enough to look about for other meeting parties. He knew most of the Special Branch men, most of them had interviewed him at one time or another but the Drug Squad was an unknown factor. Since the 'peace' the RUC had diverted manpower elsewhere, the Drug Squad inherited surveillance operators who would usually be following potential gunman. Another spin off of peace was that most of the anti terrorist operators were good, they were not easy to spot. They wouldn't fall for the 'twice round the roundabout' trick, or the 'up the dead end' ploy. Sean had attended the anti surveillance course in Donegal, and was one of the few sent to the States to benefit from the teaching of the ex FBI

47

instructor who had been friendly to both the cause and the easy dollar.

The night was dry, but cold. As he drove down the dual carriageway, descending into Larne, Sean could see the lights of the Christmas trees twinkling through the front windows of the big houses set back from the road. Only three days away was the biggest anti climax of the year. Sean had been born a devout Catholic but the troubles had robbed him of sincere feelings for any God. At least Katie would now have enough money to buy the children a thing or two. He had purchased himself a feeling of well being for Christmas. He always thought of religion as a bank balance. The first young soldier he shot as he ran across Cable Street in Derry had been balanced by the time he had refused to detonate the device under the politician's car, thus saving the lives of his two children who had accepted a lift to school at the last minute. Admittedly he had blown him up the following day, but the children were safe to mourn their father, the bank balanced, intact –

His mind drifted back to the job in hand as he saw the ferry slowly entering harbour. Sean pulled into the car park of the derelict hotel adjacent to the terminal. He got out of his car and took a stroll back to the roundabout near the vehicle exit. There was more activity than usual, many Irish families returning from the four corners of the world for the festive season. Sean had often asked himself, if the Irish are so patriotic why did so many of them choose to live on the mainland or as far afield as the States.

He had seen no obvious sign of the filth. However, he was too experienced to become complacent. In the distance he could see the flurry of activity and could hear the mighty engines straining as the ferry berthed. Two hours twenty minutes from Scotland, Sean had met dozens of ferries over the years. Especially over the last few as kids started taking a liking to ecstasy, speed and anything else that could block out reality as the music blared. The demand was proving higher than the supply. They could shift twice as much a week if they could get hold of it. Competition was becoming fierce, Seamus and his boys were breaking baseball bats on the opposition nightly. Even topping some of the main men, but there were always more willing to run the risk as the rewards were high. Patrick had approached the Dutch about who and who not to supply but they had responded by threatening to delete him from the customer list. The Dutch operated their laboratories almost openly, and they were great believers in the free market. They did not like the idea of some jumped up Irishman dictating to them. Kelly had backed off, and handed the problem over to Seamus. Seamus enjoyed his work.

The camper van bounced down the ramp from the ferry. Sean had questioned this mode of deliver during the winter months, but he had to admit to himself it did not look out of place. He could make out the tall blond bearded Dutchman driving the van. Next to him were the outstanding features of his girlfriend. In the summer Seamus had accompanied Sean on one such pickup, the Dutchman's girlfriend had been stunning in a tight white tee shirt without bra. Seamus had told everyone for days just what he was going to do to her. As usual, the camper was waved through security without a second glance. Sean walked back to his car. Out of the corner of his eye he could see the camper taking the road out of Larne. Once in his car he followed the same route, overtaking the camper on the outskirts of the town. All the way, Sean looked out for unwanted attention, but saw none. As the dual carriageway reached the top of the hill Sean turned left into the derelict garage and parked in the shadows. Seconds later the camper followed and parked next to him. Sean walked around his car as the Dutchman jumped from the camper holding an open road map flapping in the wind. To any onlooker a lost tourist asking for directions, the sight was commonplace, particularly on this road.

'How are you my friend?' Enquired the Dutchman in his faltering English.

'Fine, fine, and you and your good lady?' Sean said purposely dropping his Irish brogue in an attempt to be understand'.

'We are both in very good health, but we must hurry, you understand'.

The Dutchman's girlfriend appeared from the side of the camper, she was as stunning as ever shaking her long blond hair as if in an attempt to wake herself. She was almost struggling with a large icebox; she smiled at Sean as she placed the box next to his car. Sean's eyes followed her as she returned to the camper, he then unhurriedly picked up the box and placed it on the back seat of the Toyota, covering it with a blanket. He turned back to the Dutchman who was folding the map, which he then tucked under his arm.

'Have a very good Christmas my friend'. The Dutchman offered his hand as he spoke.

'You get home safely, see you in the New Year', Sean replied as he shook the hand.

The camper pulled out of the garage and onto the main road. Sean resisted the natural urge to speed off to safety and sat in the car park for several minutes, checking every vehicle that went by. Eventually, content that everything was in order, he drove towards Belfast. He saw no sign of the camper, but

SCAPEGOAT

[handwritten: FURTHER]

hadn't expected to. In the summer they had put a team on the Dutchman who had turned off towards Ballymena and Coleraine to make more deliveries. *[handwritten: He had sussed the team and lost them etc]*

Several miles on Sean turned left onto a farm track. He stopped for a few minutes to check his rear view mirror. Once satisfied he drove up the bumpy, crated muddy track. At the top he entered a dark farmyard and parked next to a small outbuilding. A man came out of the building, opened the rear door of the car and removed the icebox. Not a word was spoken. Sean pulled the vehicle around in a tight circle and headed back down the track and continued his journey. Another job done. It would be a similar task tomorrow morning when the overnighter berthed from Liverpool at Belfast Harbour. A different courier, a different source. Patrick Kelly never liked to be totally reliant on just one source of supply, and afterall, it was Christmas and the tablets contained in the false blue ice packs and lining of the icebox would probably feed the demands of only one rave party.

Sean would then take a break from his labours, the annual visit to his older brother Michael, on the mainland. He left the province for university in the early seventies and never returned, although his republican activities had interrupted his studies. The authorities locked him up whenever the wind blew from the west. He had remained in the University City by order. He was the main linkman for the Provos, the organiser, planner and executor of all jobs mainland.

—-oooOOOooo—-

'Last lap then lads, let's put some effort in!' Andy Woods shouted at his patrol.

51

JAMES RHYS ROBERTS

They had just returned from a week's leave, reluctantly. It had been a hard year and they were all in need of a good rest at home with their families, but this wasn't possible because their intrepid Captain volunteered them for everything going. Even if the men didn't want the break, their wives did. They swung their arms as they marched up the only half decent hill on the training area. All four of them carried a fully loaded bergen on their back, all had been weighed first thing that morning. They had completed twenty circuits of the area, bar one, but Andy felt he could complete another twenty if necessary. It had taken them some four and a half hours to complete, running down the back of the hill towards the assault course, speed marching the remainder. Nowhere near the record, but a respectable time all the same. Captain Thackray-Smith, tough shit or just TS as he was becoming known, had set them off earlier. He had been totally ignored by all when he attempted to engage anyone in conversation and had only joined them for the last lap.

Behind Andy was the patrol signaller Steve Moody, a tall handsome man who spoke with an accent straight out of Eton. He had no educational qualifications, but his family did have money, or so he made out. Next came the explosives man Kev Brabham. A solidly built man with a broad Yorkshire accent, who plodded on without comment, not a bead of sweat in sight. Lastly, and flagging slightly, was the patrol linguist Bob Bland. Fluent in 'a little bit of Arabic', bad language and German Army marching songs. He was perhaps the worse ever student in the study of the foreign tongue, although rumour had it that he had cut a few out in his time. All four had been together in the same patrol for almost three years. Both Andy and Bob had come to the Regiment from the Para's and had known each other

SCAPEGOAT

there. Steve had escaped from the Lifeguards, apparently before he was sacked for various misdemeanours, one of which had been to successfully portray himself as the new Unit Doctor for the Officers wives 'well woman' clinic. (Apparently the authorities had failed to prove it was him, but he claimed that at least three of the wives had recognised his touch).

Kev had come to the regiment from the Engineers. All his life he had taken great pleasure in blowing things up, or doing a 'Monica', as he recently started to call it. He was rated as one of the best explosives men in the Regiment. He rarely spoke, but when he did most people listened. Bob was feeling rough as he had been locked in his local pub until late the previous night and had conveniently forgotten about today's session. After the first lap he disappeared into the woods. He caught up with them on the second lap, stinking of stale lager. Andy said he had 'eyes like a badgers fanny, little pink slits'. Bob had answered him by throwing up again, this time on the march. They ran down the hill for the last time, stopping at the Landrover parked by the back gate.

Back at the Lines, as the camp was known, they all sat round recovering. They had all just emerged from the shower and were ready to go again, drinking that was. Bob was already half way down a can of cider, his brother in law worked in the local brewery and was a steady source. They laughed and talked about anything and everything. Andy opened his locker to select what he called 'his attire'. The choice was easy as there was only a pair of jeans and a shirt in there.

'Those were the days'. Bob proclaimed pointing at the photographs taped to the inside of Andy's locker door. Andy pulled the picture from the door and studied it.

'Panty Ridge, Malaya 1974 if I'm not mistaken'. Andy passed

the photo to Bob.

'Cor, I look young there', Bob looked down at his stomach and back at the photo. 'And I've hardly put any weight on over the years'.

'Let's have a look', asked Steve as he grabbed the photo out of Bob's hand. 'No I agree, you were fat then, you haven't changed at all'.

'It's not fat', added Bob grabbing the folds of his waistline. 'The doctor reckons I've got reverse anorexia'. Bob slurped back the remains of the can of cider.

'Who's the other chap? I'm sure I know him' Steve asked, looking at the other figure standing next to Andy in full jungle gear.

'You should know him you tried to get off with his missus at my wedding, remember?' Andy was dressed now.

'Oh yes, strong bastard had me by the throat'. Steve rubbed his throat as if it still hurt.

'My best man, he's going to be a copper now, took redundancy. It won't work, he lived for the Army, he should have come to the Regiment'. Andy took the photo back and slowly taped it onto the door. He had wanted to attend the Dining Out but they were on standby for the next month and confined to the Hereford area. Andy pulled a comb through his hair.

'Out for a pint tonight lads?'

'Do MPs take late night walks on Clapham Common?' replied Bob.

They all left and went their different directions.

Andy felt guilty that he had not made the effort to get to Ralph's farewell bash, but to get a stand in just to go on the piss was considered unprofessional. To send the non-availability

SCAPEGOAT

signal had been the safest option. If Ralph had found out that he was home in Hereford he would have hounded him to attend. But he still felt guilty.

—-oooOOOooo—-

Another log landed in the ashes of the large open fire, sending sparks jumping into the hearth. Kelly sat deep in the antique leather of his favourite Chesterfield armchair, looking through the goldfish bowl of a brandy glass in his hand. Late evening was his best time, his thinking time. He looked across the room at his girlfriend, Annie. It still created a stirring in his loins every time he looked at her. She was lying on her stomach on the warm double sheepskin rug in front of the fire, reading one of her magazines as she idly painted her fingernails ruby red. The short flimsy dressing gown had ridden up exposing the briefest of black G-strings cutting into her firm buttocks. She was a far cry from the walking advert for lypo suction that he used to call his wife. He hadn't seen his wife for over two years and harboured no desire to lay eyes on her ever again. The standing order at the bank and enough threats to frighten the Pope would keep her quiet.

He had found Annie serving drinks in a back street bar in Dublin and had fallen hopelessly in lust. Luckily her elder brother was a dedicated volunteer so it had been a formality to recruit her as his new 'housekeeper.' She had revitalised his fifty plus years and they had enjoyed several weeks of illicit frolicking every time his wife was out of the house. His wife had known and it came as no surprise when she had been told to pack her bags. In many respects she had welcomed the news. They had not lived as man and wife for over two years, not even sharing the same bed. He had insisted that her snoring kept him awake. She had long since resigned herself to her existence, if anything his latest orders cheered her up. The money was generous, the little house to the north of Armagh was comfortable. The threats had been totally unnecessary, she knew the way her husband worked. She knew how cold and callous he could be. Over the years she had purposely distanced herself from all his dealings, but had often overheard her husband ranting and raving. She knew his commands always resulted in another statistic in the newspapers the following day.

They had first met when Patrick, a young volunteer on the run, had taken refuge in her parent's farmhouse in the early seventies. Why he was there was never discussed. She could recall it was the week before her sixteenth birthday when he had arrived in the dead of night. She hadn't seen him for days, but was told she would have to cancel her birthday party without any explanation except, 'because of the visitor'. Patrick had started to court her one Sunday morning when her parents were at church. She had taken him a cup of tea in his room. As she placed the cup on the small bedside table, gently, not wanting to disturb him, his hand had reached out and grabbed hers. She had been pulled onto the bed and only allowed to leave when he had finished with her. She had cried, and Patrick had laughed at her. This had set the pattern for the rest of her married life. She was convinced that she would not have seen him again but for the fact that she had fallen pregnant. Her parents had blamed her and Patrick had agreed with them, but being an honourable man he told them he would stick by her. Annie rose on all fours, bottom towards Patrick.

'I'm off to bed, are you coming?' She asked in her most sultry voice. 'No, you go ahead I have a few wee jobs to see

SCAPEGOAT

I too'.

Patrick emptied the remains of the vintage brandy, put the glass down and reached for the telephone. The brassy blond walked slowly from the room, she was learning when her presence was not required.

'Seamus me boy, you well?' Patrick stood and walked about slowly as he talked. 'Yes, yes, but remember the little job we talked about the other evening, the rearranging – yes, that's the one. Why don't you get a few lads together and do that one tonight.' Patrick paused to listen to the reply, walking across the room and looking through the patio doors that led to the swimming pool.

'Listen, I don't fucking care if you are on a promise tonight, you will do as you are fucking well told – you hear me?' He pushed in the aerial of the phone and threw it onto a nearby sun lounger by the pool. Seamus had a habit of getting under his skin, in fact every bodies skin. He dropped his dressing gown by the edge of the pool and dived in sending a bow wave crashing noisily against the sides. He surfaced in the centre of the pool and rolled onto his back. He was not a man to worry, but his future seemed in turmoil and he needed to take control of it, he liked his life style and in order to maintain it he needed to be one step ahead.

--oooOOOooo--

'Bastard, one day I'll sort that bloody man!' Quigley said to no one in particular as he stood at the bar. He pushed the mobile phone back into his inside pocket. The evening had been good, up till now. The beer had flowed freely and his efforts to chat up the young American tourist searching for her Irish roots were nearing fruition. Now he had to go to work, some other fucker would get in where he left off.

'Jimmy, get the boys together, we've a job to.' Seamus said to man standing next to him at the bar.

'You have got to be fucking joking Seamus, surely.' Jimmy didn't want to play either.

'Shut the fuck up. Outside in five bloody minutes, right!' Seamus looked him straight in the eye as he spoke in order to confirm his sincerity.

He lifted the drinks from the bar, made his way back to the woman sitting at the table and made his apologies. Yes, his Ma was sick, but he would be back in an hour or so. As he walked towards the exit he could see a young stud making his way to his empty chair, next to his empty woman. Perhaps he would sort him later, If he got chance. As he left the club he had to smile as it was exactly the sort of trick he would have pulled. All's fair in love and war he thought as he hit the cold air of the night.

Once outside, standing on the pavement, he lit a cigarette and turned up the collar of his jacket. The car parked across the road started its engine and pulled over next to him, the rear door opened as it came to a halt. He jumped into the front passenger seat, Jimmy and two other burly characters walked from the club and squeezed into the rear seat. After several attempts to close the back door, they succeeded and the car sped off towards the motorway.

'This is like a sardine packers fucking outing,' One of the newcomers complained.

'What a way to spend Christmas Eve.' Jimmy added.

'Stop fucking moaning, we'll be back within the hour.

SCAPEGOAT

Lisburn.' Seamus aimed the last direction at the driver.

The windows were steamed up and smoke filled the interior of the car. They were parked opposite a nightclub in the centre of Lisburn. Seamus opened his window slightly and took stock of the situation across the road illuminated by the flashing neon lights above the entrance to the club. Young people of all shapes and sizes were queuing to gain entry. A bouncer wearing a long black overcoat over a white shirt and bow tie controlled the drunken revellers. The tall dark man was fully involved with his task.

'There's some cracking young fanny in that queue, look at the tits on that one in the white dress.' The talent scout in the back seat observed.

'She's sixteen, if she's a fucking day, jail bait she is.' Jimmy added.

'You mean too old for you – is it, Jimmy?' Quigley looked back as he spoke.

'Aye, the only thing Jimmy doesn't like about licking a bald fanny is putting the nappy back on.' All laughed, except Jimmy.

'Fuck off you lot, you'll get me a bad name.' Jimmy wasn't embarrassed.

'Once the piss heads are in we'll make our move,'

Seamus pulled a thin black nylon motorcycle balaclava over his head as he spoke, leaving it to sit like a polo neck. The others, including the driver, followed suit without being told. The queue opposite was down to the last half dozen punters.

'Right, drive round the corner, don't pay no attention to the fucker as we pass'.

They passed the bouncer and turned right into a small street, drawing no attention. Seamus turned and addressed the three in the back.

JAMES RHYS ROBERTS

'Once out, you two stagger round to the front of the club and fuck the bastard about...Jimmy you and me will get the bats and do the bastard, OK?'

'No problem; they answered in unison. They had done this type of job many times. The joking over there was now an air of seriousness. Each knew his role, compared to a bomb run or shooting this was a piece of cake. As throughout the world, bouncers are usually involved in one scam or another. This individual used to work in Belfast; for them. He had switched workplace and employer. He was now the competition. The beating would not be life threatening, but neither would it be pleasant. It was meant as a message. A loud message to be received by everyone who saw the bouncer on his crutches when he eventually left hospital. Jimmy handed a baseball bat to Seamus. They could hear a commotion as they rounded the corner of the club and could see the bouncer with his back to them, deep in conversation with their two colleagues and their drunken problems. Seamus took the first swing hitting the overcoat on the right collar with a thud. Jimmy quickly followed this with a blow to the right knee that felled the bouncer. The sound of wood on flesh and bone echoed about the street, the bouncer lay in a heap. Their two associates started to kick the injured doorman. He tried to curl up in a foetal position but he was too late, several times boots hit him straight in the face and blood and teeth showered onto the pavement. Seamus stood watching, smoking a cigarette as the proceeding continued for a minute or two, then he spoke.

'That'll do.' Seamus threw his cigarette in the gutter and walked to the front of the bouncer. Everyone knew the score, one lifted his right leg as the other stood with one foot on his chest. Seamus took a step back and swung the baseball bat

SCAPEGOAT

hitting the man in the knee. The bouncer lost consciousness before the same procedure could be repeated to the other knee. Jimmy moved the victim onto his side, they didn't want him to choke on his own blood, (considerate bastards at heart). They walked back to the car at a deliberate, arrogant pace.

The car and crew returned to the Republic club, they had a clear return run from Lisburn. An RUC traffic car stopping a drunken-driving farmer from Portadown was the only security force presence they saw. How times had changed, a year ago they would have been forced to split up and return in separate cars, even then they would have probably been arrested just for being who they were and being out of their area. Seamus liked the peace, as long as it didn't go on too long. They entered the club together, they always did, making a statement, they were still in business, still in charge. Everyone knew who they were, and what they stood for. They ruled by fear, not respect. Most people despised them, although non-dared to admit it. The task had taken them just over an hour. The American woman had gone with her stud, he decided he would sort that out tomorrow but he still found it amusing. He shouted to the barman for a dram as he reached into his pocket for his mobile.

'Santa has delivered, but he'll need a lot of wrapping paper for his present.' He snapped the mobile shut and pushed it back in his pocket then reached over the bar for his glass.

—-oooOOOooo—-

Water dripped from Kelly's head onto the phone as he listened to Seamus's efforts to be cryptic. He pulled on his silk robe as he walked back through the glass doors towards the log

61

fire. Standing in front of the fire he allowed the heat to dry him as he looked into the flames. From behind him Annie approached, naked, with a fresh brandy for Kelly in one hand, and a towel in the other. He turned to face her accepting the large glass. She gently dried his hair for a moment.

'Are you sure you're not coming to bed, darling?'

He didn't answer as she dropped to her knees and started drying his legs. Kelly felt the robe being parted and looked down as Annie buried her head between his legs. He took a large mouthful of brandy and washed it around his mouth as her head started to rock back and forth. Having swallowed the fiery liquid he threw the glass into the fire which caused a small burst of flame. He took the blond head in his hands and joined in.

—-oooOOOooo—-

Ralph had always liked Christmas at home, especially since the children had been born. Up until now he had been strong, he had preoccupied himself with work, playing cards or just getting pissed. Alcohol numbed the senses. He had been on morning shift rising at five and rushing to get into the station for the briefing at six. It had been a boring day slogging around on foot in the City centre, a perk of being a probationer. He still enjoyed the job but the paperwork was soul destroying. A shoplifter who pleaded not guilty would require a file that might take two hours to complete, then you got called the Olympic Flame - never going out! He was only surviving financially by cushioning his expenditure with what remained of his redundancy money, which was diminishing rapidly. He found a new pub, away from his home, not far from the nick.

Several nights previously he had sought shelter from the

SCAPEGOAT

weather in a doorway and was surprised to hear the strains of a fiddle through the pouring rain. The next day he was off duty so he carried out a recce. Ralph felt at home immediately, he had obviously spent too long serving in the emerald isle. Owens was a family run pub. Mr Owen was nearer eighty than seventy, with two sons in their mid thirties. They served a perfect pint of stout, dark cool body and a creamy white top. Though Ralph remained anonymous, he made this his local. The main disadvantage was the distance from his house. The first night he had fallen from the bar he had paid over twenty pounds for a taxi, he couldn't afford to continue spending that much. He thought of getting a flat in town, but this might send a message to Margaret that he didn't want her back, and he did.

He finished at two, changed his clothes and made his way to Owen's. He was off for the next two day's, so he had a session in mind. It was the last Friday before Christmas so the pub was full of office types having a final fling before the holidays. Ralph pushed his way to the bar, the barman recognised him and started pouring his pint. The pouring was a ritual, not sloshed into the glass as in some pubs. He was passed his pint, paid for it and found a corner where he wouldn't be buffeted about. Music drifted in from the small bar at the back. Any musician could walk in off the street and join in, as long as his or her music was good. Drinks donated by the public encouraged them, a bad music player went thirsty and didn't stay long. The walls of the bar were festooned with Irish regalia ranging from wooden shilalees to embroidered maps depicting everywhere from the Mourne Mountains to the Giants Causeway. He sank the first pint quickly and pushed to the bar for his second.

'Cheer up me boy, its Christmas, remember.'
The voice came from a greying man Ralph had noticed several

times before. The man introduced himself as Michael and extended a hand that Ralph managed to shake through the crush at the bar.

'Have a beer Ralph, make the most of it I only buy at Christmas'.

'Go on then I'll have a stout'.

Once they were served they moved back to the quiet corner, Ralph noticed Michael was drinking orange juice.

'On the wagon are we', Ralph pointed at the other mans glass.

'Yes, regrettably, my stout days are over, I flew a little too close to the wind, never did know when to stop. Going to die of fucking orange juice poisoning now'.

Ralph took a swig of his pint.

'You work round here Ralph?' Michael enquired.

'Yes, moved up from Nottingham the other week'.

'Nottingham, I went there once, five women to every man. I think my five were on holiday that weekend, what line you in?'

'Insurance, household, life, in fact anything'.

They continued to chat for an hour or so, Ralph got gradually pissed and Michael sipped at his orange. Michael excused himself and disappeared to the gents, he was followed by a monster of a man with collar length black greasy hair. Once in the toilet the man pushed open the lavatory door to confirm they were alone.

'Whose yer man Michael?'

'I'm not sure, no panic he's harmless, but we'll check him out before too long.'

—-oooOOOooo—-

SCAPEGOAT

    Sean left Belfast without ceremony. He walked briskly into the City centre carrying a small grip containing the essentials of life; toothbrush, spare shirt and underwear. Once in the melting pot of the crowds and satisfied he didn't have company, he jumped into a taxi and headed for the airport. The peaceful times had seen general security slacken throughout the system, Sean however, remained vigilant, and embarked upon one of his circuitous routes. Once at the airport he purchased a single ticket for the imminent departure of the Paris flight. Having paid in cash he made his way to the departure lounge. Peace or no peace the duty special branch man had clocked him on camera the minute he had entered the terminal, Headquarters in Belfast were informed of his destination. Sean rarely drank but ordered his mandatory- 'I'm away from it all'- gin and tonic as the aircraft ascended through the clouds. As he looked out of the small window down at the lush green of his homeland he wondered whether he was losing his direction, his cause. He had not joined the people's army all those years ago to deal in drugs, organise intimidation and fight turf wars. Yes, he thought to himself, he needed to get away. Once in France he caught a taxi to the Gard Du Nord and joined the queue for the shuttle train. A few hours later he changed trains in London and headed north, his second gin and tonic rattling on the table in front of him.

    No red carpet at the large Victorian railway station, no red carpet as he made his way through the rain to the warmth of the public bar. As he entered the bar he immediately registered his brother sitting exactly where he had been last Christmas. Had he moved since? Sean joked to himself as he turned to the bar for his third gin and tonic. An arm came round his shoulders and his older brother gave him a strong but emotional hug.

'Nice to see you me boy, good trip?'

'Yes, uneventful as ever.' Sean turned and followed his brother to his seat.

They sat and talked generally for several minutes, covering everything from Margaret's fracas with Seamus to Patrick Kelly's new swimming pool. Michael shook his head in disbelief on being told about the latter.

'And what's wrong with you my 'deeper than the oceans blue' little brother?' Michael looked purposeful at Sean.

'Nothing, well nothing I can put my finger on. Well nothing and everything I suppose'.

'Go on, bounce it off me, you usually do'.

'Back in the seventies I followed your lead, not blindfolded. I stood back and looked at the situation, who was right and who was wrong. I had no doubt in my calling, we were getting shat on from all directions. No jobs, not even an interview if your address was anywhere near the Falls'. Sean paused searching for the right words.

'And now you've lost direction?'

'No, I haven't, but every bugger else seems to have. With Kelly and his like disinfecting themselves after one of their occasional visits to Belfast. More interested in the profit from dealing in drugs, porn and God knows what than the cause. I'm not sure I belong anymore'.

Michael put his hand on his brother's shoulder in support, and leant nearer to him.

'Don't think for a moment that it hasn't been noticed, not a bloody moment. You are strong my boy, strong in faith and strong in patriotism. Stay that way. The likes you are talking about will be sorted don't you worry. Nothing has escaped

SCAPEGOAT

Dublin, the likes of Kelly don't run the show, and they'll find that out when the time suits. You just see my little brother, you just wait and see'.

With that the older man slapped his brother on the shoulder and stood up which halted the line of conversation abruptly.

'Let's be home for some food'. Michael said as he led his visitor from the bar.

CHAPTER SIX

Ralph had been on duty for two hours. He was in the hit squad, the van crew, cracking jokes and breaking wind was the order of the day. Their task was to respond to pub fights and public order situations, but in reality they were just dogs bodies collecting shoplifters or attending to burgled cars. Ralph preferred this to plodding the streets aimlessly. The radio crackled and the officer in the front passenger seat turned on the siren as they raced across town to settle what a landlord had reported as a riot. When they arrived every man and his police dog where in attendance. Apparently two gypsies had been caught cheating at cards and someone had glassed the pair of them. The offender had legged it and no one seemed bothered. 'He's done the world a favour', seemed the general consensus. The paramedics were inserting drips, the police officers were talking about everything but the situation. Ralph overheard one of the dog men identifying both of the gypsies as known troublemakers. One, the dog man claimed, had stabbed a copper a few years ago and got away with it. As the stretchers passed Ralph he immediately recognised both of them, pity he hadn't been first to arrive at the scene he thought, there would be no use for any drips.

'Come on Ralph, another shout!'

A voice called from the van. The Christmas spirit was obviously being taken liberally by all. Again they sped off through the streets, sirens blaring at the shoppers.

'Owens, the Irish pub,' the call came from the front.

'Shit!' Ralph thought, hoping it would be cancelled before they arrived. He did not want to blow another pub, especially this one. They pulled up outside to be met by the landlord. All was in order they were told, the offenders had been 'seen off'. Ralph knew that trouble wasn't tolerated in this pub, the police were never involved.

Inside the bar Michael sat quietly as ever. He had made sure the two dickheads who had decided to push 'an old paddy' about had been sorted by the monster who had grabbed them by the necks and banged their heads together. Michael stood and looked through the window as the police van pulled off. Inside the van Ralph allowed himself one sneaky look at the pub. He had kept his head down throughout their visit, he didn't see Michael behind the curtain, but Michael saw him.

—-oooOOOooo—-

The streetlights reflected through the heavy, cold rain from the numerous water filled potholes of the car park. The dark hatchback was well hidden in the shadows at the far end, as the large Irishman picked his way through the minefield of water towards the vehicle. As he approached the car the driver's window wound down, the monster put his head to the opening. Having heard what was said he retorted.

SCAPEGOAT

'Are you sure, not the Branch or any other bastard?'.

'No, just a joe crow, ex squaddie, probationer – nothing sinister'.

The monster didn't waste time, having passed the roll of notes to the CID men he walked back across the car park splashing through the deep puddles. He hated squaddies more than he hated bent fucking coppers.

—-oooOOOooo—-

Around the corner just a few hundred yards away stood Ralph, a cold, wet, and thoroughly pissed off police officer. He was stopping vehicles and checking documents with a Sergeant and three other, equally unimpressed, officers. Checking documents was the legal excuse to catch the drink drivers battling their way home from their office parties. Up to now they had had no success, but the man running the show was keen as the rain did not reach into the shop doorway the Sergeant had selected for himself. Ralph stood in the road and raised his hand in an attempt to halt the oncoming silver BMW, ever ready to dive out the way in case he failed. The large car, over dramatically, screeched to a halt.

'What the fuck you trying to do, Babylon?' The dreadlocked black man shouted in a high-pitched voice.

'You gonna get yourself killed white boy!' He turned to the white Blonde girl who sat next to him.

'Sorry Sir, perhaps if you drove a little slower, more carefully'.

Ralph embarked upon his training school politeness. The Sergeant appeared to be paying not the slightest notice, even though he was to write Ralph a performance report after the patrol. He seemed more interested in the blonde's breasts.

'Just a routine vehicle documents check Sir, won't keep you a minute'.

'Won't take that long Babylon cause I ain't got my fucking papers – so get the producer done, I got better places to be'.

The black man grabbed his girl by the hair pulled her to him and pushed his tongue deep in her mouth, all the time looking at Ralph and the rain dripping from his helmet onto his nose.

'Name, Sir?' Ralph asked, pen poised.

'Nathaniel Jason Campbell, date of birth ten, nine, fifty four – eleven A, Chapel Hill, Shirefield, England'. The man had obviously been stopped before.
Ralph completed the form and the talk that went with it.

'Before you go Sir, I'll just check you out, have you been in trouble with the police at all'.
Before he got chance to answer the Sergeant had come to life and pulled Ralph to one side.

'Don't bother son we're finished here, let him on his way'.
Ralph paused, thought better of rebelling, and turned back to the driver handing him the form.

'Right, thank you for your co-operation, have a safe journey.' The driver took the form and threw it on the back seat. Ralph could see that it joined at least two other similar forms plus several parking tickets. The black man smiled as he wheel spun away in the rain. The police officers followed the Sergeant back to the station.

'Take your meal break now.' The Sergeant instructed as they entered the nick.

'Ellis, have a quick scoff and be in my office in half an hour, OK?'

'Yes Sarge.'

SCAPEGOAT

Ralph managed to suppress his urge to tell him exactly what he wanted to say. Ralph was too angry to eat, he ran up the stairs to the third floor and the snooker room.

Several other officers entered the massive room accommodating three large green tables, Ralph was smashing balls into pockets on the centre table.

'Fucking niggers,' Ralph said to no one in particular. 'They get away with fucking blue murder, and not one senior officer has got the bottle to do anything about it!'
Ralph sent a ball flying off the table and across the floor. All the other officers made to concentrate on their sandwiches or chips, no one wishing to join in a debate of this nature. Ralph knew it was pointless attempting to provoke conversation, the issue of racism was flavour of the month, every month, twelve months a year. He didn't consider himself a racist. Ralph just deplored the way yobs in the black ghettos were allowed to go their own way. Late night illegal drinking clubs, drug dealing, robberies and rapes. If it happened within the Chapel Hill area, it happened. There wasn't one senior officer who was willing to provoke a riot and subsequently destroy his career just to lock up another black. So went life.

Ralph looked at his watch, rested his cue on the snooker table and made his way to the Sergeants office back down on the first floor. He knocked on the door, which was slightly ajar.

'Come in'. The Sergeant was sitting at the desk eating, or trying to eat, a large kebab. His blue jumper covered with various items that had missed his mouth, it also bore the stains of previous fallen items. A shining example Ralph thought to himself.

'Close the door and take a seat Ellis, I won't be a second'. The kebab was finally devoured, the chin wiped with the sleeve of the jumper. The Sergeant picked up the papers from the table to his front.

'I thought I had finished your report Ellis, but I must admit I have my doubts'.

'Doubts, Sarge?'

'Yes, doubts Ellis. When you first arrived you showed great promise. In the last months your mind seems elsewhere, your turnout is immaculate, but you personally look like shit. I know you've got your problems at home but that should not effect your work, although in fact I don't think it does, it's something deeper. Tonight on the vehicle checkpoint I had a feeling you were going to take things into your own hands, I may be wrong, am I?'

Ralph didn't answer.

'Ellis, you are an older recruit. Older people have not attended school with ethnic groups, haven't lived next door to them. They are the racists in this country and if I am not wrong you are one of them, even if you are not aware of it.' Ralph had had enough.

'No, Sarge, I disagree. It's not the colour of the skin but the lifestyle I am against. They have a total disregard for law and order. They run most of the drugs and whores in the city, and we sit back and let them do it. No one seems to have the courage to rock the boat.'

The Sergeant stood up and clicked on the electric kettle behind him.

'Ellis, you of all people should realise the potential of chaos. Remember when the army thought it would be in Ulster for a few months. Twenty years later and over two thousand lives lost, its still there. This whole country is a tinderbox, one spark!' Ralph decided to nod in agreement and get back to playing snooker. The Sergeant continued.

'I haven't made mention of this aspect in your report but have no doubt I will be watching you in the future.' The Sergeant passed Ralph the report. 'Read it, and sign it in the usual place.' Ralph hardly bothered, having flicked through the pages he scribbled his signature and stood up.

'Is that all Sergeant?'

The Sergeant nodded and Ralph left the room without further ado. Behind him the Sergeant made his cup of coffee, deep in thought. He could sense trouble and he was usually right.

—-oooOOOooo—-

The pub was as lively as ever with music pounding out from the back room. Sean looked across the bar at his older brother who was in deep, serious conversation with the monster. Michael returned to the table.

'Sorry about that, no rest for the wicked.' Sean took a swig of his beer.

'Problems?' Sean enquired.

'No, well I don't think so'.

Michael went on to explain about the drinker who was an insurance man, but was really an ex soldier who was now a policeman. Sean knew better than to advise his brother, he had a great respect for the thoroughness of Michael's investigations. The conversation moved onto the new peace and the way ahead. Sean mentioned Patrick Kelly's intentions to control the peace; Michael had never liked Kelly but had to admit the man had vision. Someone who was blessed with a fine singing voice was hitting the high notes of 'Four Green Fields'. The bar, including the two brothers, hushed in appreciation.

JAMES RHYS ROBERTS

As the singer finished his sad rendering the audience burst into applause. The eyes of grown men were watering, most of the Irishman present would much rather have been at home. For some this foreign soil had become home, many just wanted a peaceful existence and would have no truck with the ideals of the terrorists. Michael appeared to be miles away.

'Missing home at last?'

'No.' Michael replied.

'Mr Kelly's idea, I enjoy the challenge of finding a solution, leave it with me for a few days'.

Sean knew that his brother enjoyed a mental challenge, he had no doubt he would come up with a plan, but it wouldn't be easy and for him to get involved would be the ultimate challenge. If there were any mistakes Kelly would make sure the shit landed firmly back at the feet of the man with the original idea whoever that might be. Kelly was good at that. On the other hand if it succeeded Kelly would revel in the glory, as he had often done in the past.

—-oooOOOooo—-

Back at the nick Ralph finished his shift with an hour of drinking time to go. He was offered overtime to cover for yet another female ringing in with a sore stomach, but refused it without a second thought. The whole shift had been a stressful experience, he just wanted to get to the pub and hopefully get locked in. He could have been sensible and returned to his house, but the thought of pushing open the front door to all the unopened brown envelopes depressed him. His bank balance was now critically low, he solved the mounting debts by not touching the envelopes. The, I can't be skint, I've got cheques left

76

SCAPEGOAT

syndrome.

Ralph was changed and walking towards the strains of Four Green Fields within minutes. Invitations from his colleagues to join them for a Christmas drink across the road were ignored. What did he have in common with most of them, nothing, he thought to himself as he strode up the road. He left school when he was fifteen, in fact he had hardly made an appearance in his last year of school. Some of his shift had left schooling last year, albeit with a degree or two, they were still doing the same shit jobs as he was, on the same shit pay. Ralph had long since decided that to get on in the police he had to be a black, pregnant lesbian, with six fucking degrees and a gay boyfriend. He needed a pint, no – several pints.

As he pushed into the bar the doors hit the mass of bodies behind them. Head down he quickly ferreted his way through the throng to the bar. Michael had clocked his arrival straight away and jumped out of his seat, Sean thought the Pope had popped in for last orders.

'I'll get that one!' Michael called to the landlord.

'Cheers, Michael, it must be Christmas that's the second one this year.' Ralph took the first, long swig as he spoke.

'Come and join us Ralphie, you must meet me brother.' Ralph drank as he followed Michael through the crowd. Sean stood up as they approached.

'Ralph, Sean – Sean, Ralph.' Sean took Ralph's hand and shook it hard. Ralph was surprised at the strength of the insignificant looking hand.

'Good to meet you, Sean is it?'

'Yes Sean, Michael has mentioned you, and he's bought you a drink, you must be important.'

'No, just a second rate insurance salesman.' Ralph continued

77

the farce.

'And you Sean, over for Christmas?'

'No, I live in Paris, left Ireland many years ago. The troubles you know, not a nice place to live. You ever been there?'

'Where, Ireland? Only once to Dublin, for the rugby, nice place.' Ralph turned away hoping to kill the subject. Sean took the hint and changed the topic.

'Finished work for the holidays?'

'Yes, no more quotes, claims or final demands for a whole bloody week.' Ralph emptied his glass.

'Anyone for a drink?,' he offered. No one accepted so he made his way to the bar and ordered two pints, sinking one as he waited for the other to be poured.

He's quite convincing.' Sean whispered to Michael across the table.

'Lies with confidence, too much bloody confidence.' Michael replied.

Ralph returned to the table and continued the small talk. Michael made his way to the bar and quietly had a word with the landlord. On his return to the table he shared the news that they were to be locked in, and that Ralph as one of his friends, was more than welcome to join them. Ralph accepted without hesitation.

The drink flowed freely. Ralph and Sean sat quietly, happily lying to each other; Sean about his mundane existence in Paris and Ralph about the vigour of the insurance world. When the landlord started cleaning the tables around them they knew it was their hint to depart. By this time, Ralph was well pissed,

'Back to my place,' invited Michael.

Ralph, Sean and the monster followed Michael back to his house.

As drunk as Ralph was, he found himself quite surprised

SCAPEGOAT

at the large town house in which Michael lived. He wiped his shoes on the doormat before following the rest into the hall. The pictures and books everywhere did not seem to suit the ex alcoholic Irishman, but Ralph was just glad of the company and a chance to continue drinking.

'Happy Christmas,' declared Sean as he passed Ralph the large glass of whisky.

Ralph realised it was now the early hours of Christmas Day, shit! He hadn't sent any cards, or any presents to his children. Between work and drinking he had managed to occupy all his time and mind. He took another large mouthful of whisky and made a mental plan to get to Wales, somehow, later in the day and see his kids. He then emptied the remains of the glass and accepted a refill. He was comfortable. He had sunk deep into the soft armchair and Irish ballads drifted across the room on the smoky air. The conversation was low and meaningless as he fell into a deep sleep; Sean caught the glass as it fell from his hand.

Quickly and effortlessly the monster picked up Ralph from the armchair and carried him up the stairs. Seconds later he returned with Ralph's wallet and bunch of keys. As Sean took impressions of the house keys in a bar of soap, Michael emptied the contents of the wallet onto the table.

'PC 141 Ralph Ellis', Michael read aloud from the police warrant card.

'A member of the Parachute Regiment Association, Colour Sergeant Ellis, 2nd Battalion the Parachute Regiment', he added after reading another card. Sean gestured to the monster.

'We'll go and have a look at the house.' Michael nodded in agreement and both men left.

As the front door slammed Michael made his way upstairs to

the spare room. Ralph lay on his side, not just asleep but unconscious. Michael stood over the bed, deep in thought

Sean and the monster made their way to Ralph's house. On arrival they used a key to open the front door. Sean stumbled over the pile of mail inside the door. They closed the curtains and switched on the lights. The monster stood guard in the hall as Sean moved about the house. In a corner of the front room, was a bureau. Above it, mounted on the wall were various framed photographs. Central was one of a younger Ralph, his arm around a woman and two children at their feet. Around this family picture were other frames that captured a pictorial history of Ralph's life. There was one of a youthful Ralph kneeling next to the biggest silver cup in the world. In para-smock, maroon beret and with self-loading rifle. The engraved brass plaque proclaimed 'Champion SLR Shot – Bisley – 1972'. Other pictures showed Ralph parachuting, skiing, or just being a soldier. One in particular caught Sean's eye. This one had clearly been taken on the Falls Road, Ralph ,with rifle resting on his hip was in the centre of a group of fellow paratroopers. Sean read in a whisper, 'Internment 1973'. Sean had been shot and injured during internment as he narrowly escaped being incarcerated, unlike many of his friends, many of them not involved in the IRA. Well, not until then. Sean was taking a dislike to his brother's houseguest. Before leaving the house they steamed open some of the letters from the hall. They then locked the door and returned to Michael's.

On their return they reported all they had discovered. Michael was particularly interested in the contents of the mail.

'Looks like our boy here is well in the shit then,'

'Yes,' Replied Sean, 'Debts up to his fucking eyeballs, and the CSA are chasing him.' 'What do you reckon, Sean' Sean

SCAPEGOAT

replied without hesitation.

'Waste of a bullet really, let's just throw him in the river.' Michael thought for a minute.

'You've been working with Seamus for too long, no, we'll sit on PC Ellis for a while.'

'And if we have no use for him?' Sean enquired.

'Then we'll put him where he belongs.'

—-oooOOOooo—-

Many hours later Ralph woke to the smell of fried bacon and eggs. For a moment he didn't have a clue where he was. He took a minute to run himself through the night before. He could remember the lock in and leaving the pub, but from there on things were a little hazy. He took in his surroundings as he lay back in the small single bed. The room had no window but the door was slightly open allowing the noise and smells from downstairs to drift in. On the walls were four or five old, expensively framed oil paintings. On the opposite wall was a large bookcase packed tight with old books of various sizes. Ralph heard footsteps approaching across the landing.

'Oh! You are alive then – fancy a wee bit of breakfast?' asked Michael.

'Yes please. What time did we get back here?' Michael looked at his watch.

'About four o'clock I think it was, and you were on good form.'

Michael walked back down the stairs and Ralph attempted to get out of bed. He was still fully dressed, his shoes neatly placed beside the bed. As he sat up he thought he might pass out, he cradled his aching head in his hands. He started to remember that it was Christmas Day when he felt an incredible pain in the pit of his stomach. His hands moved to clutch the pain but as he did he realised that the source of the pain was about to leave his body. He staggered to his feet and rushed out onto the landing, to his right he saw the bathroom. With seconds to spare he managed to push his head into the toilet bowl just as a great gush of vomit sprayed from his mouth. He heaved and heaved, the gush became a dribble, and the dribble became droplets. He wanted to die. He slowly realised that standing behind him was Sean, wanting to help.

'Feeling rough?' He enquired.

'Nothing that a hair of the dog won't cure.'

Ralph stood up, wiped his mouth with a piece of toilet paper and pulled the flush; he didn't want to lose face. He pulled more toilet paper from the roll and made an effort to wipe the bowl and flush it again. He then turned and washed his face in cold water straight from the tap. Finally he rinsed his mouth after squirting a length of toothpaste into his mouth. Ralph felt like shit as he descended the stairs pulling a comb through his wet hair. At this moment in time food was the last thing on his mind, he needed a drink. He put on a brave face as he entered the kitchen.

'I hear your stomachs gone down the bog, come and get some breakfast down you.'

Michael was wearing a novelty apron making him out to be a French waiter complete with bow tie; he pulled out a chair in invitation to Ralph. Ralph sat down and was confronted by a full Irish breakfast of two eggs, sausage, bacon, soda bread and potato farls. He took one look and was tempted to run back to the toilet. All four of them, Ralph, Michael, Sean and the monster started eating. The monster was shovelling his mountain of

SCAPEGOAT

calories down his throat, Michael talked more then ate; Sean picked at his food and stared at Ralph. Ralph put a morsel in his mouth and waited patiently to see if his stomach would accept it. Within minutes he couldn't even look at his food let alone eat it. He pushed his plate away. No one mentioned his lack of appetite.

Shortly afterwards they all made their way back to the pub for a repeat of the day before. They entered through the back door, as the bar was not open to non-regulars. Ralph downed his first pint in seconds; all thoughts of his children, presents or Christmas went out of the window. After about an hour, to Ralph's surprise, Michael and Sean said their goodbyes and headed for the door. The monster remained, but he never spoke anyway. The other punters were bedded in for the afternoon so Ralph took up post at the corner of the bar and drank himself into a stupor. In the early evening the landlord told everyone he was closing, Ralph staggered out into the cold evening. The monster appeared out of the shadows and asked him if he wanted a lift anywhere.

'Fucking hell it spoke!' Ralph exclaimed.

The monster was a patient man, 'one day,' he thought to himself, 'one day.'

Ralph accepted the lift, spent a quiet journey home and told the monster to drop him off round the corner from his house, thinking he was being clever. He pushed the front door open and almost fell inside, kicking the pile of mail out of the way. He managed to slam the door behind him, found the front room and collapsed onto the settee in a drunken heap.

83

CHAPTER SEVEN

Michael and Sean had purposely backed off from Ralph. Michael needed time to think. As they and the monster sat eating breakfast it was Michael who spoke first.

'We can use this man, but for what and when is beyond me. I think that when in doubt of what to do, to do nothing is the best course of action. He ain't going nowhere.' Sean was between mouthfuls of breakfast.

'I take it we can find out all there is to know about him?'

'Yes, that'll be no problem.'

Meanwhile, some twenty miles away, Ralph was waking to face the day. As usual he felt like shit and was still fully dressed in the clothes he had left the nick in two days ago. He rolled of the sofa and walked slowly into the kitchen. He looked around for something to dry up the alcohol in his body; the bread in the wrapper was starting to go green. He sat patiently pulling the bits of mould from the bread before placing what was left of two slices into the toaster. He made himself a mug of coffee and drank it black because the milk refused to pour from the bottle. Once the toast was done he sat at the small table eating slowly and looking around at the mess. He hadn't cleaned the house properly since his wife had left. There were four black bin bags in the corner of the room; the sink was overflowing with pots. He had been drunk last night, but normal drunk, not like the night before. He was attempting to grasp reality, it was Boxing Day, and he realised again that he hadn't been in touch with his children.

He reached for the telephone, but found that the line was dead. He hadn't paid the bill; it had been cut off. He threw the handset across the room. He decided to have a sort out, he place an empty bin next to the table and went out into the hall, returning with arms full of mail. For the next thirty minutes he separated the rubbish from the bills and other mail. The result depressed him. In addition to the telephone bill, the bank had not paid the mortgage for the last two months, there were several letters reminding him and warning of the possible result. A letter from his bank manager, the letter some two weeks old, demanded his presence. It highlighted that Ralph's income did not even cover his standing orders, never mind his other spending. He had two choices, ring the bank manager and sort things out, or go on the piss. He decided he needed a shower and a change of clothes before he went back to the pub. As he drove back into town he passed a car sales showroom, it was open. Twenty minutes later he drove away in a small, rusty motor. He knew he had been ripped off, but he also knew he had funds in his pocket. His plan had been to get some money into the bank, but he needed a drink first.

oooOOOooo

'Steam was better.' Michael pronounced as the-inter city

SCAPEGOAT

locomotive pulled into the station.

'You're just showing your age.' Replied Sean, bag in hand, his visit over. Michael was not the sentimental type; in fact he didn't usually see his brother off but he was getting older and age always seems to make people more considerate. Sean was going back to a land of no consideration, at least not amongst the type of people he associated with.

'Have a good journey. I don't know why you don't go direct, it's peace now you know, all finished.' Sean turned as he walked towards his train.

'I don't think so.' Sean got on the train and disappeared from view, Michael was already walking away.
By the time Michael arrived at the pub Ralph was on his second pint.

'Orange, Michael?'

'I don't mind if I do, when you back to the grind then?' Ralph ordered the orange juice and another pint for himself.

'Another two days and back to the trials and tribulations of the insurance world.'

'Aye, the insurance world,' repeated Michael as he walked over to his usual table.
Ralph joined him without being invited.

'Sean not out today?'

'No, he's away back to Paris won't be seeing him till next year now.' Michael seemed sad and withdrawn. Ralph thought that Michael's sombre mood was because his brother had left, so they drank in silence, neither feeling conversation necessary.

—-oooOOOooo—-

JAMES RHYS ROBERTS

In the hills above Ballymena stood a large white house with a gravel driveway leading from the road. At the entrance was a small gatehouse, complete with hidden cameras. Behind the lace curtains of the gatehouse sat one of the security team, pistol on the table in front of him. His partner would be patrolling the grounds, they would take it in turns throughout their tour of duty. They were quiet, dedicated men. They viewed their duties as a privilege, not a chore.

In the main house, in bay window of the library, stood a tall grey haired man, a glass of good red wine in hand. The walls of the room were lined with rows and rows of dark wood shelves housing books of various shapes and sizes. On any occasional expanse of un-shelfed wall were large stuffed salmon or items of antique fishing equipment. The security man patrolling the grounds looked up towards the big house as he weaved his way through the trees and bushes of the gardens. The grey man nodded acknowledgement, the patrolman raised his hand in return.

'We must try to give these men a break from their duties. They do us proud, year in and year out'
The younger man sitting across the room stood and joined his father at the window.
'Father, with the peace and all we'll be lucky to have any security at all soon.'
'Over my dead body. There will never be peace for the likes of us, not when murderous mobs are being released from jail. The fight to remain British has never been more difficult, especially now. The British don't want us anymore. It'll fall to you to continue the battle, I won't be around for ever.'
The younger man put his arm around his fathers shoulder.

88

SCAPEGOAT

'Don't be so melancholy, you're as strong as an ox.' The older man took a long drink from his wineglass.

—-oooOOOooo—-

Ralph was tanked up again. He staggered from the pub down the road towards the Police station where he had parked his car. He couldn't recall when Michael had left him, it had been some time ago. Ralph had stood at the bar and drank and drank, he now felt sick. As he approached the station nausea took control and he leaned against the nearest wall as he threw his heart up. At that precise moment Inspector Hardy chose to open the window of his third floor office in order to have a cigarette, the sound of Ralph's retching drew his attention. Another drunk, he thought. Another waste of space on his way home to beat up the wife, he should really send someone to arrest him, get him off the streets, but he just couldn't be bothered.

The drunk finished his task, wiped his chin and continued on his way. After a few steps he stopped, unzipped himself, and pissed against the wall. The Inspector tutted to himself and finished his smoke, then just before he closed the window he noticed the drunk was on his way again. Much to his surprise he watched as the man walked into the station yard. The Inspector walked to another office and watched from the window as the drunk let himself into a parked car and climbed into the back.

The Inspector approached the car gingerly, but noticed the station car pass displayed in the window. He shone his torch into the back of the car onto the face of the sleeping drunk. He didn't know the name but he recognised the face as belonging to one of the probationers from another shift. Situations like this

JAMES RHYS ROBERTS

always resulted in drama, experience had taught him that. The Inspector's radio came to life requesting his presence in the Charge Office. As he walked away he made a mental note to follow this up.

A police siren sounded, waking Ralph with a start. It was daylight, and as was usual lately, he felt like shit as he peered through the steamy car window at the outside world. There was the occasional police officer going about his business, but it was generally quiet. Ralph grabbed his bag from the front seat of the car and quickly made his way into the building and up the back stairs to the gym, where the showers were. He quickly shaved and showered and attempted to turn himself back into something resembling a human being. As he combed his hair he realised that he started night shift that evening. He needed a drink. He looked at the hand that held the comb, the shaking was more than noticeable. Ralph knew he had a day to get his act together and not have a drink, it would be difficult.

As he descended the stairs he turned into, and almost knocked over, the night shift Inspector.

'Ah, PC Ellis isn't it?'

'Yes Sir,' Ralph replied.

'Good night last night was it?'

'Yes Sir, a party, an old Army friend.'

The Inspector continued his climb up the stairs,

'Well don't forget the booze will still be in your body, I'd breathalyse myself before driving if I were you.'

'Yes Sir, I'll take that advice, thank you sir.'

Ralph stood still for a moment. He hadn't wanted his social life known and he knew that too many things were going wrong. He also knew that the Inspector wouldn't leave it at that, they never did. The canteen seemed a good idea, just to kill some

SCAPEGOAT

time if nothing else. The idea of a big greasy breakfast did not appeal to him, so he settled for coffee and some toast but ate only a mouthful of the toast and sipped at the coffee.

Back in the car park he noticed that all the night shift cars had left, he felt safe that the Inspector had also left and so quickly got into his vehicle and drove off towards home. On the third floor, civilian jacket over his white shirt, the Inspector was making yet another effort to leave the station. He looked out of a window as he waited for the lift and just caught the back end of a vehicle he knew. He made a mental note of the time.

--oooOOOoo--

Sean grimaced when he saw Quigley waiting for him as he entered the arrivals lounge. He had planned to get a taxi as he usually did, to delay a meeting with Quigley if for no other reason.

'A good trip to merry old England?' Quigley enquired in his best Oxbridge accent.

'Fuck off!' Replied Sean.

'Mr Kelly requires our presence. We're to be honoured with lunch at the Ponderosa.'

Quigley followed Sean as they walked quickly from the concourse. Out of the corner of his eye Sean could see cameras following their progress. As they reached fresh air Quigley overtook Sean and guided him towards the waiting car. The driver started the engine as Quigley dropped into the front passenger seat. Once Sean was seated in the back the car moved off.

'Kelly's place.' Quigley instructed.

As the car bumped over the tarmac mounds at the vehicle check point the telephone rang in the Special Branch office of the terminal.

'That's them out of the airport, they have taken the road south, not to the city.'

The silent journey ended as the car moved slowly up the gravel track towards the big house. As they approached, Kelly stepped through the large front doors to welcome his guests.

'Good to see you Sean, how's your brother?'

'He's fine Patrick. He sends his regards.'

'Come in, I thought we'd have a spot of lunch, and talk some business.'

He turned and led the way through the hall and into the dining room. Laid out on a large mahogany table was lunch, consisting of plates of various meats and large bowls of salad. A bit different from the chippy they usually use, Sean thought to himself. Seamus waded in, piling food into a small mountain on his plate. What he couldn't catch with his fork he just grabbed with his fingers. Sean picked a few items from the remaining debris.

'We're under pressure, Dublin are demanding action and we need a plan. I was hoping something would fall in our laps, but not this time. I have to admit I'm fucked for ideas.'

No one spoke until Seamus, with a mouth full of chicken leg grunted.

'Just let me and the lads off the leash Mr Kelly. We'll go and top half a dozen orange bastards, they'll retaliate and we're back in business'

'Seamus if you had a brain you would be fucking dangerous, I told you we want no comebacks. If any action lands back on our doorstep we'll be lynched, even the Catholics want us to

SCAPEGOAT

hand back our weapons. Sean, you usually have the ideas?'

'There's a man in England, my brother found him, or he found my brother.'

Sean went on to explain about the insurance salesman, who was really a peeler, who was also an ex-Para.

'How we could use him we're not sure; or how we can get him to do what we want. But he may be of use. Just maybe.'

Kelly wanted to know more. In fact every detail. Sean quickly attempted to dampen his enthusiasm but Kelly was desperate to satisfy Dublin and would not listen.

'I'll be talking to your brother Sean, he needs to get a plan together and quick.'

Sean knew what he would do. All of a sudden it would be, Michael's idea, Michael's plan and possibly, Michael's fuck up. Not Kelly's. Seamus made an intellectual contribution, spraying coleslaw as he spoke.

'Trust a fucking Brit, not only a Brit but a fucking Para, Mr Kelly come on.'

'Seamus, shut the fuck up!' Was Kelly's intellectual reply.

The conversation moved onto local business, which meant drugs, beatings and money. Seamus soon became bored and wandered from the dining room through to the swimming pool. Music gently drifted from the speakers mounted on the walls as the long slim body of Kelly's girlfriend cruised up and down the pool. Seamus stood by the door drooling, the young girl smiled invitingly towards him, he returned the smile. The water dripped from her body as she pulled herself out of the pool, the tight bikini clinging to her firm young breasts. Seamus moved forward to offer a hand.

'Seamus, get back and finish your lunch, and you get some

fucking clothes on.'
Kelly threw her a towel and turned to follow Seamus back to the dining room.

'Seamus.'

'Yes Boss.'

'Don't ever be tempted to cross the line, or you will be very sorry.'

'Yes Boss.'

' Sean, Ring your brother, tell him to be at the alternative phone at eight tonight. Don't be tempted to give as much as a hint, not on his line.'

'No problem Mr Kelly.'

Sean placed his plate on the table as he spoke and turned to Seamus who was still stuffing his face.

'We off then?'

Seamus grabbed two chicken legs from the plate and continued eating them as he followed Sean from the house. Kelly stood at the door as the men got back into the car.

'Don't forget Sean, another pickup tomorrow at Larne.'

Sean nodded acknowledgement and the car drove off towards the City, his dank flat and a world light year away from Mr Kelly's Xanadu.

CHAPTER EIGHT

Ralph managed to keep himself busy all day, he even tidied the house. The days of drinking had taken their toll, he hadn't eaten a proper meal for nearly a week. He looked in the mirror as he shaved. There were dark bags under his eyes, which had sunk into his skull, and he craved a drink. Luckily there was no alcohol in the house. He had managed to stop himself going out to buy some, but only just. He had an hour to get to work. He finished shaving again and threw on a tracksuit; his uniform was hanging in the locker at work. No officers at Shirefield commuted to work in uniform. It was only a year since an officer had been beaten into a coma while waiting for a bus. His children had not recognised him when they visited him in hospital. Ralph pushed the new mail away from the front door as he left, twenty-five minutes later he parked in the station car park he had awoken in in less than ten hours before.

The briefing went on and on. The Inspector gave details of all the incidents that occurred during the Christmas period. Tomorrow was New Years Eve and trouble was expected from every quarter, but tonight he was on foot patrol on his own, which suited the way he felt. He left the station without needing to be prompted and turned his collar up against the fine rain as he walked out through the back gate. He would hide. Not sleeping or totally avoiding his duties, he would just find 'the route of least resistance'. A phrase used by one of the better members of the shift one cold and boring night as they sat in a patrol car and solved the problems of the world. Until an unsociable burglar who, duty dictated, had to be chased and caught had interrupted their debate. The rain gradually turned into sleet, and then on into snow. Ralph had a constant pain in his stomach which seemed to be aggravated by the smell of beer. Each time he approached a public house he took the precaution of crossing the road.

Midnight approached and Ralph had, so far, achieved his aim. He had not used his radio once. He was wondering how much longer his peace would last when he heard his number being called. The control room ordered him and the other officers on foot patrol to return to the station. He acknowledged the instruction and made his way back to base. As he entered the yard he saw a hive of activity, officers he didn't know were throwing riot kit into the back of various police vans. He was told there was a briefing in five minutes and made his way up to the second floor. Sitting around a large table were about twenty officers, mainly male and big. He knew only three or four from his own shift, the others were from the Support Unit.

A grey haired man in a leather jacket and jeans entered the room and took centre stage.

'Gentlemen, and ladies.'

He noticed the females at the last moment.

'We have a quick, hopefully peaceful job to do. As most of you are aware our Afro Caribbean friends on Chapel Hill have

opened yet another illegal drinking club. Our job is to pay it a visit, and advise them about the laws regarding such establishments.'
He paused and looked around the room.
'This is not to be a heavy-handed hit, we want no arrests, no riots. We are just telling them we know what they are doing, does everyone understand?'
There was a silence then Ralph spoke.
'Sir, what if they refuse to leave the place, surely we can arrest a few then?'
'No, no and no again. As I said there will be no arrests, if there is trouble we back off. If they start to leave, let them go. If they refuse to go, we go. I know it's frustrating, but believe me it's a means to an end.'
The man didn't ask for questions again, he just walked from the room. A sergeant from the Support Unit shouted.
'Let's have you down in the vans, you people giving us a hand spread yourselves amongst the four vehicles.' Ralph was wound up again. He felt like shit and could do with a drink, on top off that he was off to give kid glove treatment to a load of blacks.
'If they were white we'd bloody pile in,' Ralph commented as he walked down the stairs with the other officers.
No one replied. Once in the station yard Ralph physically checked that he had his favourite toy; his telescopic carbon steel baton. He took it from his belt and flicked it open to check it.
'You can put that away son, you won't be using that tonight.' The Sergeant said as he walked past him.
Ralph said nothing and collapsed the baton by hitting the point on the tarmac. A last check to make sure he had his pepper spray and he jumped into the back of the nearest van. The

Support Unit lads were in good spirits and laughed and joked amongst themselves. Ralph was an outsider and was ignored. The Police van convoy left the City centre and made it's way up Chapel Hill.

As they approached the illegal drinking club they could hear the bass sounds booming out. The first van turned into the street and a few black youths that were standing outside the club quickly moved inside. Ralph was bemused by the total disorganisation. No one had been told exactly where to go, or which area was their responsibility and no one seemed particularly interested. All four vans were now spilling their passengers outside the entrance to the club, the Sergeant shouted orders left, right and centre. The police officers jogged into their given positions, Ralph stood by the van feeling like a spare prick. The Sergeant noticed him and as almost an afterthought told him to cover the rear of the building. Most of the Support Unit had been instructed to enter the premises, Ralph was very surprised to find he was the only officer at the back of the building. Inside, the music inside stopped abruptly, followed equally abruptly by loudly shouted orders.

Ralph stood near the only rear door to the end of terrace house. The house next door was bricked up but, judging by the noise from inside, it appeared that the club had been extended into this building as well. Many minutes passed and Ralph began to get cold as well as bored. Again he checked the position of his truncheon and gas. He was fantasising about swinging the extended metal rod when he heard noises from inside the door. He steeped back and drew his truncheon. The wooden door swung violently open and a large black figure appeared, stumbling as he ran. Ralph saw the dreadlocks and features of someone he had met before; someone he had prayed to meet again on

SCAPEGOAT

a dark night like tonight.

'Looking for your BMW are we Sir?'
The black man stopped in his tracks. Ralph racked the baton making the sections clunk firmly into position.

'Hey look man, stay cool, just do as you were told.'
The black man had lost his Rastafarian accent. Ralph took no notice, he had made his mind up what he was going to do and the red mist had taken over. The black man managed to put his arm up to protect his head from the incoming carbon steel. The bone snapped, clearly audible. Ralph took a step back and swung again, this time hitting the man on the left knee felling him like a tree. The black man looked up in pain, helpless as Ralph raised the truncheon above his head. Someone appeared from the side of the building.

'What the fuck are you doing!'
It was the Sergeant. He leapt towards Ralph and grabbed the weapon from his hands. The Sergeant looked down at the black injured figure.

'Oh, shit! Now you've done it. Get back to the van, what's your name?'

'PC Ellis.' Ralph seemed in shock and walked slowly away as he spoke.

As he walked back to the van he was overcome with nausea, he couldn't understand why. He leaned against the wall of the house vomiting as officers from the Support Unit ran past to assist the Sergeant. Ralph eventually arrived at the van, removed his helmet and sat inside. He ran his hand over his forehead and found that although cold he was sweating heavily. Within minutes an ambulance arrived and the injured man was loaded onto a stretcher. A dozen or so black youth's started shouting abuse and two or three bottles were thrown. The

JAMES RHYS ROBERTS

Sergeant appeared and ordered everyone into the vehicles. As the officers were boarding the vans more blacks spilled from the club swelling the numbers already outside. More bottles were thrown, one hitting the windscreen of the first van sending glass flying in all directions. The driver took splinters full in the face but was aware of the danger and bravely attempted to complete the retreat. This proved both a bloody and painful task, also an impossible one. As he rounded the corner one of the glass splinters found his eye. His hands came up to comfort the excruciating pain, the van veered out of control and struck a low wall. A high wall would have served to guide the vehicle on it's way, the low wall managed to help the van turn slowly onto it's side. Inside was a chaos of riot shields and helmets falling onto officers who were lying in a tangled heap.

The black youth's cheered their success, and continued hurling bottles as the officers attempted to crawl from the stricken vehicle. The bloodied, hapless officers made their way to other vans the lessor injured helping those more seriously damaged. Once everyone was accounted for all four vans left the area. They had gone only a short distance when a loud bang followed by a tower of flame and thick black smoke marked the end of the fifth van. Sirens blaring they raced back to the Station. As soon as they pulled into the yard injured people almost fell from the vans. Ambulances started to arrive and deal with the devastation. Ralph stood by his van, mesmerised. In his mind Ralph was back in Ajax Bay watching Welsh Guardsmen crawl onto the shore. Legs missing, faces still burning. The Sergeant grabbed him by the arm.

'You better come with me before my men get to you, come on.' Ralph complied like a lamb.

SCAPEGOAT

The Sergeant led him to the third floor of the Station and sat him in an empty office. The Sergeant then left the room, closing the door behind him. Ralph was in a daze, he could hear talking outside in the corridor. The door opened and the Sergeant entered followed by the shift Inspector.

'Ellis, can you hear me?'

'Yes, Sir!' Ralph answered in a military manner.

'Relax Ellis,' the Inspector sat on the chair next to him.

'I have no intention of discussing this matter tonight. Shortly you will be taken home. Consider yourself suspended, do you understand?'

He received no reply.

'Your Warrant Card.'

The Inspector put out his hand. Ralph took his wallet from his pocket and placed it in the empty hand. The Inspector took the warrant card from it's display leaf in the wallet and offered the wallet back, but received no response and finally thrust it into Ralph's jacket pocket.

'Stay here until you are told otherwise.'

Again Ralph failed to acknowledge the instructions and sat head down looking at the floor. Both the Inspector and the Sergeant left the room and closed the door. Once out of earshot the Inspector turned.

'He's not with it, is he?'

'Either that or he's being very clever. But I think you're right Sir, he's got a problem that' for sure.' They both continued on their way.

Sometime later two PC's Ralph didn't know came up to fetch him. A silent journey to Ralph's home followed, Ralph went into his house sat in the big armchair and switched on the

JAMES RHYS ROBERTS

tape recorder on the table next to him. As he sat in the dark, his mind in turmoil, the carnage of earlier in the evening failed to penetrate his thoughts; he was miles away, years away. As the ballad on the tape filled the room Ralph stared into the darkness, tears rolling down his cheeks.

CHAPTER NINE

Somewhere in the darkness was a ringing sound, it got louder and louder as Ralph tried to ignore it. The ringing of the doorbell was followed by banging; the combined sound managed to annoy him enough to rouse him from his deep sleep. He rubbed his face with the palms of his hands in an effort to wake himself and made his way to the front door.

'Hello,' he managed, weakly.

'PC Ellis, we haven't met I'm the local bobby. I have a message from Superintendent Fathers of Complaints and Discipline Department; you are ordered to attend the Assistant Chief Constables office at three o'clock, full tunic – do you understand?' Ralph couldn't get his head around what was being said.

'Er, Yes, yes mate.'

'They are going to send a unmarked car for you at two o'clock, do you understand?'

'Yes, yes course I do.' but Ralph was not totally with it.

The bobby turned on his heels and walked back to his car. Ralph shut the door and made his way into the front room, he flopped into the chair, almost falling over onto his back. His mind debriefed him slowly on the happenings of the previous night. He concluded that he was in for a mega-bollocking. So, he had smacked a black, there were no witnesses, he had threatened him. A knife, yes, a knife. Had anyone searched the area; doubtful? He had pulled a blade tried to stab him. Bollocking my arse, a pat on the back more like it. Feeling a 'Commendation' coming on Ralph jumped up from the chair that had served as a bed all night and made his way into the kitchen. He filled the kettle and put it on to boil, black coffee again, the milk was now a strange shade of green. He was beginning to feel better, the drink was nearly out of his system and the sleep had done him good.

He sipped at his coffee as he ironed a clean white shirt, his tunic and trousers were in the suit carrier and were still immaculate from his passing out parade after training. He found his army boots which were bulled and looked like black glass, he gently wiped the dust from the toecaps. He laid out his uniform, medal ribbons adding the final touch. Taking a roll of tape from a draw he took a length and rolled it around his fingers, sticky side out. From the cupboard he took his second helmet, this one hadn't been kicked about by drunks on a Saturday night. With the tape he brushed the material till the newness returned. Once he was satisfied he placed the helmet in a clean carrier bag. He shaved and showered quickly as the time was getting on, as he stood under the shower his mind went through his convincing saga of the black man and the knife. Why hadn't he mentioned it last night? Shock, that'll be it, some sick leave then. Once dry he put on his uniform, admiring himself in the mirror as he dressed.

A car horn sounded outside. Time had flown by as he had prepared himself for the praise he was about to receive. He threw on a civvy jacket, picked up the carrier bag containing his helmet, and his jacket in its suit cover. He made his way to the

SCAPEGOAT

waiting vehicle. Inside were two plain-clothes officers, he didn't recognise either. Ralph got into the back of the car and said his hellos; he didn't get a reply, the journey into the city was silent. Eventually they pulled into the underground car park of the headquarters building; Ralph quickly put on his jacket and helmet. The two officers led the way from the car park, up a back stairs and along a long corridor. One of them knocked on a door but didn't wait for an answer before opening it, he held the door open and beckoned Ralph forward. Ralph made a few final adjustments to his uniform and marched in. As he turned into the office his step faltered and he drew to an untidy halt. In front of him was a large dark wooden desk, behind it sat an equally large senior officer with more medal ribbons than Ralph and a lot of silver braid adorning his uniform. The office was huge, the far side a small conference centre complete with table and chairs. Around the table sat more officers of various ranks and sizes, Ralph recognised the one who had given the briefing the previous night. The Support Unit Sergeant was also there, and others he did not know. The officer behind the desk stood up.

'PC Ellis let me make you aware that this gathering is an extraordinary Disciplinary Tribunal. Your Police Federation representative is here to see the rules are adhered to, as are all the witnesses to last night's incident. Before we go any further I'd be very interested in hearing what you have to say about last night.' Ralph launched into his well-rehearsed story.

'Sir, I was ordered to cover the rear of the building on my own, there were no other officers near me. After a few minutes the back door burst open and this black guy came running towards me, with a knife...'

'A knife?'

'Yes Sir, a knife in his hand....'
There was a knock on the door, the braided officer walked across the room and opened it. Ralph almost choked. In walked the black man from the previous night. His left arm was in a sling and he limped badly.

'PC Ellis, let me introduce Detective Sergeant William Hardy, Regional Crime Squad, the one with the knife?'
There followed an icy silence throughout the room.

'Sergeant Hardy was, until last night, deep undercover within a yardie gang. For your information it had taken DC Hardy, at great risk to himself, nearly a year to gain their trust. I have a good mind to allow DC Hardy to repay your efforts in culturing community harmony, but we don't work that way – regrettably.' The injured officer was helped into a seat.

'Last night's operation, which you managed to turn into a bloody disaster, was an effort to re-route a large shipment of crack cocaine. An effort to get the goods where we could hit them without causing a riot. But your conduct, PC Ellis, fucked that plan right up and put lives at risk to boot.' Ralph knew when to speak and when not to, this was the latter.

'PC Ellis, you are to leave the force, do you understand?'
'Yes Sir.'
'We can take two roads, both lead to the same result. Road one, you resign. You go, minimum paperwork and the possibility that we can keep the drug operation running. Understand Ellis?'
'Yes, Sir.'
'Road two, we charge you with assault, we send you to jail, then we throw you out of the force. Understand Ellis?'
'Yes Sir.' 'The Federation representative will give you advise if you are thick enough to need it.'
'No Sir, that won't be necessary.'

SCAPEGOAT

'Right, sign here and here.' Ralph took the paperwork and the pen and scribbled an excuse for a signature.

'Ellis, you are no longer a police officer, you will return home with the two officers who brought you here. You will hand the officers all items of police uniform and equipment, your locker at the station has already been emptied. You will receive your last salary cheque at the end of the month. Do you understand?'
Ralph was again in shock. He felt as if he were riding an express train to unemployment that he could neither slow down nor stop. So much for a pat on the back.

Ralph followed the officers to the car and sat quietly for the return journey home. Once there he filled two black refuse bags with his uniform and handed them over. The officers remained silent and without emotion. When they left Ralph closed the front door behind them and heard the car drive away. There was yet more mail at his feet, and in his present condition it was all too much for him, but he needed to busy himself, so he picked up the mail, headed for the kitchen, and made himself some coffee.

It was all bad news, he couldn't even make sense of his bank statements. There were final demands and mortgage reminders, all too much to handle at this moment. He snapped and threw the coffee across the room. The cup smashed into a thousand pieces and the coffee splashed up the wall. He grabbed his car keys and headed for the door fastening the buttons on the shirt he had put on after unceremoniously handing his uniform over. 'It's not right', he thought to himself, 'it should have been like the telly, should have had my buttons ripped off and my sword snapped.' As he drove away from the house he felt a weight lifting from his shoulders; after all, it was only a job.

    He parked the car on wasteland some distance from the pub and headed for oblivion, via the cashpoint for beer coupons. The machine failed to recognise his dilemma and gave him two hundred pounds, but Ralph knew it was only a matter of time before the financial rug would be pulled from under his feet. He pushed his way through the teatime office types and took position at the bar. Michael had clocked him as he entered, he sensed something different about Ralph. 'There is a God,' thought Michael. Having not seen Ralph for days he had become a little nervous. The phone call from Belfast had the backing of Dublin, Michael had checked that. Ralph needed to be worked on and fast. The way he was downing the drink Michael wondered whether his little squaddie friend would survive to serve their purposes

    'Long time no see.' Michael pushed in beside Ralph.

    'Michael, my friend, have a drink.' Ralph was already slurring.

    'Go on then, I'll take an orange juice.'

    'An orange juice for my friend, and make it a large one!' Ralph was well on his way.

    'What are you celebrating Ralph, you seem a bit different.'

    'You're right there Michael, I am different. I am now one of the many unemployed. Apparently the insurance world can do without me, and to be honest I can do without it.'

    'I'm sorry to hear that Ralph, I'm sure you'll find something else.'

    'I only wish I could share your confidence, I only wish.' Ralph drained his pint and started on the fresh one waiting on the bar. Michael made his way back to his seat whilst Ralph continued his trip away from the ever growing problems of reality.

    The time for last orders arrived, much to Ralph's annoyance. He called another two pints and a large whisky. He was on the brink of an abyss, he was mumbling to himself and he had to force down his throat the liquid he had purchased. He left the last pint untouched and staggered out into the night air, Michael watched him go but made no attempt to communicate with him. Ralph was back on the drink and Michael knew from experience that a drinker with money in his pocket wouldn't stay away from the bar for long. He would catch up with Ralph tomorrow, he had work to do before then. He made for the door, the monster followed shortly afterwards. Michael walked straight to the phone box opposite the pub, luckily it hadn't been used as a urinal tonight. He dialled a number, waited a few seconds, then replaced the handset and lit a cigarette while he waited. The phone rang loudly.

'Resigned, that doesn't sound right, had to resign, that's more like it.' He replaced the handset without further comment.

    Ralph woke early in the morning on the backseat of his car, he could not recall the journey from the pub. He was frozen to the bone, the car was covered in a coat of frost. He tried to sit up but the pain in his head forced him back down. He could smell his own breath, it made him make a second attempt to sit upright. This time, with his head held in his hands, he made it. He opened the car door and slid gently into the cold morning air. The car acted as a support as he took a much-needed piss, not caring who might be watching. A women in a business suit walked passed and shot Ralph a look of disgust as she saw what he was doing. Ralph stuck his tongue out at her.

'The pair of us are unemployed now.' Ralph mumbled to himself as he looked down and fastened his flies. He slammed the rear door of the car and staggered off to find a café and a hot coffee to defrost his body. His usual was open so he sat in the corner cupping a mug of steaming coffee and looking aimlessly at the condensation running down the window. He needed a drink.

Michael spent the morning using his mobile phone. The telephone in his house was not to be trusted, (he even changed his mobile every other month), he knew the security services were constantly monitoring his movements and communications. He confirmed through his police contacts that Ralph had indeed resigned from the force, under a cloud. His contact was finding it hard to confirm the actual circumstances of Ralph's downfall, but apparently it had something to do with a raid on a black drinking club. It was only a matter of time before every detail filtered down, policemen being policemen the canteen would eventually hear all the nitty gritty. Ralph was now more vulnerable than ever, albeit not in a position to be exploited as yet, but that would be arranged.

After scraping the frost from the windscreen of his car Ralph had managed to drive home. He parked on the drive and walked towards the front door.

'Mr Ellis?' A voice stopped him in his tracks.

'Mr Ellis, I am a certified Bailiff acting on behalf of Ferguson Finance. Apparently they have sent you four letters regarding your HP commitments specifically a washing machine, a fridge and a television.'

'Fuck off.' Ralph retorted and turned towards the house. The well-built bouncer type character was joined by a human rottweiller type character who had been sitting in a white van parked across the road. They knew their job and timed it so that Ralph had unlocked the front door before continuing.

'Mr Ellis.' One man had followed Ralph into the house and now was in a position to block any effort to close the door.

'Mr Ellis, we have a job to do, it's nothing personal.'
Ralph just couldn't be bothered, he stood aside and allowed the men to walk through and remove the electrical items they wanted. They emptied the fridge throwing the few contents onto the worktop, a lump of green furry cheese nearly bit one of them. Ralph sat in the kitchen and stared into space, the large man returned and thrust a form and pen under his nose. Ralph signed it without reading or paying any attention to it. He heard the van pull away and went upstairs for a change of clothes and a shower. The shower ran for a few minutes as he undressed. Inspecting himself in the full-length mirror he was surprised at how his gut was developing. Gone was the six pack he had been cultivating since his youth, his muscle volume was depleting, he could see himself going to seed but was past caring. If he started to think about everything that had happened since he left the Army his mind rebelled. This was the man who could out run anyone, out shoot champions and drink the best under the table. What had gone wrong.

He entered the shower and let out a loud. 'Fucking Hell!' It was freezing; he jumped out and wrapped a towel around his waist. The pilot light had probably blown out on the boiler; he went back down the stairs to check. He was wrong, the gas supply had been turned off. Probably one of the many brown envelopes he had chosen to ignore. He lifted the phone to give someone a mouthful and get his heating back on but the phone line was dead, he had forgotten it was the first casualty of his financial crisis. Returning upstairs he walked back into the cold shower and swore over and over again at the invisible bureaucratic enemy. He dried and selected some clean clothes from the dwindling few, plugging the iron in he noticed the light didn't come on. It was the last straw, no gas, electric or telephone – temper took over and the iron smashed against the large picture on the wall above the bed sending glass everywhere. Ralph put the clothes on as they were and stormed from the house.

Ralph walked eagerly into the bar, it had only just opened so it was quiet. Michael was sat in the corner and allowed himself a sly smile as he could feel a plan come together. Predictably Ralph launched into another session standing on his own facing the bar and ignoring all those around him. As the hours rolled by he could be heard talking quietly to himself. Early evening Ralph staggered out followed seconds later by the monster who shadowed him to his car and watched as he collapsed into the back seat. Michael was looking after a valuable commodity, the monster took position in the dark shadows of a nearby doorway.

After about an hour the monster's attention was drawn to shouting, in the distance, but coming in his direction. He pulled back further into the shadows. Seconds later two local yobo's appears from around the corner. Wearing the mandatory sports kit and baseball caps they made a beeline for Ralph's car, one keeping watch as the other tried the door handles. Discovering the back door open the would-be thief beckoned to his accomplice. They saw Ralph, unconscious and quickly took advantage. The first man leaned over Ralph and started going through his pockets. The monster moved slowly and unnoticed from the shadows. The searcher passed his henchman a wallet followed by a watch. As he started to empty the wallet onto

SCAPEGOAT

the roof of the car the monster grabbed him by the back of his head and drove his face into the cold metal. As he collapsed to the ground the first thief shouted.

'What the fuck!' And made to move out of the car, only to meet the incoming fist of the Irishman full in the face.

The Monster made a call on his mobile and within minutes a van drew up and the two still bodies were thrown into the back. Ralph's wallet and watch were collected from the frozen mud and placed on his chest before the Monster moved back into the shadows to continue his duties.

Ralph stirred much as the day before, but looking ten times worse. He was unshaven, dirty and smelly. Yet again he was frozen to the marrow. Something on his chest caught his eye, it was the gold strap of his watch. Next to that was his wallet, he panicked, grabbed the wallet and quickly checked the few pounds remaining. The notes were still there, 'strange', he thought, but put it down to the possibility of looking for something in his drunken stupor. Remembering his lesson of the day before he gently eased his body into a sitting position. As he did this he caught sight of himself in the rear view mirror and thought for a moment that a tramp had got into his car, but he was to far gone to be bothered. He was awake later today and discounted a visit to the café, doubting they would serve him in his current state. Using one of the credit cards from his wallet he scraped the ice from the windows of the car. 'About all the cards could be used for', he thought to himself. He took a piss at the back of the car, but without the audience of the previous day. Then, throwing caution to the wind, he drove towards home. The journey was uneventful apart from a short distance when a police car tucked in behind him, but they didn't stop him.

Ralph still felt drunk but managed to drive in a straight line, at least while the police car was behind him.

As he turned the car into his street he immediately saw the men around the house. Parked outside was a large flatbed lorry. All the windows of his house had been boarded up and the men were adding the finishing touches to boarding up the front door. Ralph screeched to a halt and headed for the men.

'You fucking bastards!' He screamed.
He was onto the first man, who appeared to be the boss, before he could react. Grabbing him by the lapels he pushed him up against the wall of the house.

'Mr Ellis I presume.' The suit managed to say.

'What the fuck you doing?'

'Mr Ellis, we are acting on behalf of your building society. Mr Ellis you haven't paid your mortgage for five month's, they have written to you and they have sent people to see you. They sent someone to interview you at work yesterday in a last effort to sort the matter out.'

'I don't work there anymore.'

'Yes, I know.' By now the other men had surrounded Ralph and he knew he couldn't win.

'We've put your clothes in bags and put them in the garage for you, I'm afraid Mr Ellis you are no longer allowed onto the property.'

Ralph reacted without thought, he was furious, in an instant his head came back and he had driven his forehead into the nose of the pompous bastard in front of him. The nose exploded. Blood spread over the man's face, before the other men could grab Ralph and pull him off. Ralph shook the men off, turned and walked back to his car, it would have been dangerous for anyone to tackle him in this state, the men seemed to sense this and

SCAPEGOAT

allowed him to leave. He drove back into town.

With only a few quid left he decided to try his luck with the cashpoint again, but failed, it recognised him and ate his card. He considered selling his car but on reflection decided against this as he would have nowhere to sleep. Most of all he needed a drink, food didn't enter his thought's at all. He decided to buy some cans from the supermarket and sit in the car and get quietly pissed. But then he remembered he could be arrested for being drunk in charge of a motor vehicle so he cancelled thoughts of drinking in the car and found an alleyway to hold his solitary party. After four cans he started to feel better, the second four cans had him considering entering the London marathon. The last four put an end to that idea. By now it was late afternoon and he made his way back to the supermarket, it was about to close. He selected another four pack but as he counted his money on the way to the till he realised he did not have enough. He returned to the shelves under the watchful eye of the security guard, selected and paid for a cheap bottle of Sherry, and made his way back to the alleyway.

—-oooOOOooo—-

The Monster watched as Ralph made his way for supplies and let him continue on his way. He had things to do. Within minutes he had forced the screwdriver behind the plastic housing of the car handle, he reached inside and pulled the plunger that not only opened the door but also deactivated the alarm. 'Marvellous security systems these,' he thought. Once inside the car it took only two attempts to forcefully rotate the steering wheel through the lock, off with the housing and the screwdriver was in the ignition barrel and he was away. Five minutes later he reversed the car into the lockup garage, got out, closed the double doors and placed the padlock in position. It would be a long cold night for Mr. Ellis tonight.

—-oooOOOooo—-

An hour or so later Ralph was at the staggering stage and made his way back, under cover of darkness, to where he had left his car earlier in the day. He had parked it in the same place on the two previous nights, but for the life of him he couldn't find the damn thing. 'It's the drink,' he thought as he swigged at the half empty bottle of cheap sherry.

For the next hour he wandered about getting more and more annoyed with himself over the missing car and getting drunker and drunker. He sat in the corner of the waste ground that he had parked in earlier that day. The alcohol had wiped his mind clean. At first he was convinced of where he had parked but then managed to persuade himself that it was at the station. His station, totally forgetting the fact that he was no longer a police officer. He smashed the empty bottle against a wall and wondered off towards the station. The sherry had been a last, cheap resort. It had not agreed with him, especially on a stomach that had not seen food for over two days. Totally unnoticed he walked into the police yard, the busy operators were not monitoring the cameras covering that area. Failing to find his car he fell into the nearest police vehicle, stretched out on the back seat, and fell asleep. After a few minutes his small private world started to spin, he sat up quickly and was violently sick over the front passenger seat, the final drips landed on his chest as he fell back again; this time into a deep sleep.

SCAPEGOAT

In the police station, upstairs in the snooker room, Karen was finishing a kebab. She was driving the response car tonight, which pleased her, but she had been partnered with the Inspector, which pissed her off severely. She had half an hour of her meal break left; she would usually have gone to the gym but today, as she was in the response car, she wanted to be ready to deploy. Her radio crackled.

'All officers. Alarm at Stanley's warehouse, intruder's believed to be still on the premises!'

She ran for the stairs, acknowledging the message and confirming she was attending. In the back of her mind she hoped the Inspector had missed the message so she could leave him behind, but any idea of freedom was short lived as the Inspector ran out of the Gents fastening his trousers. They ran across the yard together and jumped into the vehicle.

'Bloody hell!' Shouted the Inspector feeling his seat in the dark.

'Stop the car.'

He got out and shone his torch at the pool of vomit on his seat. His hand felt his backside; now soaking wet. The smell was appalling, Karen didn't know whether to laugh or throw up. They both moved away from the vehicle but the stench followed the Inspector. Karen reported on her radio that they would not be attending because of vehicle problems, then she walked back to the vehicle and looked in the back seat.

'Sir, I think you should see this.'

The Inspector walked towards her, a puzzled look on his face.

'The dirty bastard, lock him up!'

Ralph was oblivious to everything about him and to compound matters his bladder had decided to empty without bothering to wake him.

JAMES RHYS ROBERTS

A van arrived after a while and Karen explained the task. The two officers, who had served on the same shift as Ralph, were very impressed. They grabbed him by the feet and pulled him from the vehicle, his body hit the ground like a heavy sack. They then dragged him over to the van, roughly lifted him and threw him into the back. Luckily he felt nothing, he just groaned as he landed on the floor of the van. They drove to the charge office where Ralph received similar treatment; he was eventually put in the drunk's cell. This consisted of a wooden bed, no mattress or blankets. It was designed so that it could be hosed down once the occupant departed, unless the occupant was in a state in which case they would then leave them situ when it was hosed out. For many of the regular drunks it was the only wash they had for weeks. Ralph threw up once more during the night, onto the cell floor.

Early the following morning Ralph heard the cell door open, Karen stood over him.

'What are you like.' Ralph opened his eyes but kept silent.

'You need a kick up the arse, look at you.'

He managed to sit up, but only just.

'What do you care?' He managed to say.

'Well truth be known, I don't really, but Christ Ralph you had everything going for you and look at you now.'

He looked down at the spew on his chest and the dark damp patch about his crutch; he was definitely not dressed to score.

'Just take a little advise from a friend, stop the drink and get your shit together, or you'll end up in Peace Gardens with the rest of the wino's. You're better than that Ralph.'

She gave him a smile and a wink before turning and slamming the cell door.

It got to Ralph. The embarrassment and concern he had

SCAPEGOAT

seen on Karen's face was difficult to accept. He felt as if he were on a ledge, two thirds of the way down a cliff and it would be easier to slide over the edge into the deep sea than attempt the difficult climb up to safety. The door swung open and the Custody Sergeant walked in, interrupting his thoughts.

'What are we going to do with you?'
He sat on the end of the bed next to Ralph.

'The Inspector wants you charged and put in the morning court.'

'He would.' Ralph replied.

'Listen Ralph, you weren't a bad bobby, if fact you could have been good, but that's all history. I'm not going to charge you on one condition.'

'What's that?'

'The Police car, no one will clean it and I don't blame them. You go and wash it out and we'll lose the paperwork, what do you say?'

'OK, thanks.' The Sergeant walked from the cell leaving the door open, Ralph noticed the pool of vomit on the floor.

He washed out the cell without being asked. He then walked down the corridor leading past the desk and reception area to the exit door. As he approached the desk he saw several bobbies booking in a prisoner, the proceedings halted as he passed them. All went quiet and a younger officer took a step back. Ralph ran the gauntlet and pushed open the door to complete his escape. He was well aware that he had hit an all time low, no money, filthy and thirsty. He had promised to clean the Police car, but that could fuck off – he needed a drink. The icy January cold bit into his face as he walked up the hill, the warmth of the cell behind him. He made his way to where he had parked his car, convinced that in the bright light of day it would be where he left it, but he was wrong The wasteland stretched emptily in front of him. Now he couldn't get home to change into the clothes left in the bin bags in the garage, and he had nowhere to sleep. For the first time in his life he felt helpless, vulnerable. He continued to walk the streets just to keep warm. A short distance away Michael turned up the heat in the car as he watched Ralph walk dejectedly from the wasteland.

CHAPTER TEN

'Good leave?' Asked Steve.

'Brill, first Christmas I've had at home for years.' Andy replied. They were going through their standby kit, black overalls, respirators, smoke canisters and various ropes. They'd unloaded the Range Rover and were checking everything before reloading the vehicle. The other two men in the patrol had gone off to get the mail and collect rumours. It was the only way to find out what was going on, the head shed used security as an excuse to let people know what was happening at the last minute.

'Mail for the men!' Shouted Bob, as he returned carrying a large sack of official and personal mail.

'Where's Kev, got lost?'

'No, he's sniffing round headquarters, rumours are thin on the ground.'

Work on the sorting of equipment ceased as they followed the mail sack into the crew room. The sack was emptied onto the floor; most of it was official looking brown envelopes but there was other mail as well. As they were putting the mail into piles according to name the last member of the patrol entered the room.

'Rumour HQ seems to be closed, not much about at all.' Said Kev as he joined in sorting the mail.

'D Squadron are off to the States on parachute trials or something.'

'Jammy bastards.' Steve added. 'And they're after a patrol for across the water.' No one responded.

'Sergeant Woods!' A voice shouted outside.

'It's that fucking knob, TS'. Steve said quietly.

'Yes Sir!' Andy walked to meet his superior as he spoke. The Captain entered the room,

'What's this Sergeant, playtime? All your patrol equipment is spread over the road and you lot are sitting here gossiping. Have you forgotten it's nearly confidential report time? You lot had better pull your fingers out.'

Andy stood facing the Captain clenching his fists until his knuckles were white.

'I'll be back in an hour make sure everything is shipshape.' He spoke over his shoulder as he turned and left the building. The patrol members looked at each other, sharing a mutual bond of hatred. Andy sat down again.

'One day I'll swing for that bastard, I swear it.' Was the collective unspoken thought.

The atmosphere picked up as they opened envelopes containing Christmas cards and stood them on the table. Andy was surprised not to have received one from his mate Ralph. He was probably too busy being an officer of the law, or upset because he had not made the effort to attend his farewell dinner.

'I've got a cunning plan.' Kev said in his best Baldrick voice.

'Oh no, not again.' Groaned Steve.

'I can still remember the - let's go for a quiet pint - in Singapore, last year. I woke up in jail three days later.'

SCAPEGOAT

'No, this is a sensible idea. Why don't we volunteer, as a patrol, to do that Ireland tour that's up for grabs? At least we'll get away from TS for six months, and we can do some severe socialising.'

'Yes, we don't need to take any weapons, it's cease fire you know.' Andy added in agreement.

'Only if I can take my old MG, I can do a complete rebuild in six months.' Steve added hopefully.

'Take a vote.' Bob managed one of his rare statements.

'Okay, those for, raise your right hand.' Andy said, doing his leader bit. Everyone put up a hand.

'Motion carried.'

—-oooOOOooo—-

It was a bright, crisp, spring like day on the streets of Belfast. Sean had been out and about since early morning, Seamus, as usual, was still rotting in his pit. The slight, nervous looking figure of Sean was a common sight this early and he was greeted by many of the locals as he walked up the Falls Road. He could sense a plan coming together. His brother had phoned him from the mainland the night before and he was aware of all the various developments. Kelly had been demanding action and at last Sean had been able to start planning and give him some answers to his many questions. He made his way to Katie's house to check that all was well. Because of his lifestyle he lacked genuine friendship. His visits to Katey were a period of sanity in a far from sane world and he treasured his friendship with the handsome woman. He knocked on her front door.

'Come in!' Shouted the widow from inside.

'Sean, me darling, tea?' She kissed him on the cheek in welcome.

'Yes, please,' he took a seat as he accepted.

'You seem to be in a good mood, is it the weather, or has Quigley been shot?'

'Regrettably not, just the weather, but we can live in hope.' Laughter came flooding from the kitchen.

She placed a tray of tea, cakes and biscuits on the small table in front of Sean.

'Help yourself.'

Sean felt at home and poured himself and Katey a cup, passing hers across the table. As he sipped at the brown liquid his eyes studied the beauty of his friend, as she got older she became better looking than ever. His eyes followed her long red hair over her shoulders as it fell over her shapely breasts. Burning through the white blouse he could see the red of her nipples showing through the lace pattern of her bra. His deep friendship was rapidly becoming more of an infatuation, he snapped his eyes away in embarrassment. For a moment he had allowed his attention to slip, he felt as if he had mauled her. He gulped at his tea, almost burning his lips. The attention hadn't been lost on Katey, she had enjoyed it, in fact her bosom glowed and ached.

They both changed the subject that never was.

'I recognise that spring in your step Sean, you've found something to entertain that brain of yours.' She could read him like a book.

'In a way, but its business, you know.'

'I know, ask no questions, tell no lies.' She topped up the both cups.

'Sean, I've been thinking about, business, as you call it. As you know I live under a cloud, you know and I know that my husband was no tout and the lies and gossip I can live with, but.'

SCAPEGOAT

She took a sip from her cup, Sean sat up and paid attention.

'Well, I've been thinking about the girls growing up, I don't want them suffering the way I have that's just not fair.'

'They won't. I will see to that!' Sean promised.

'Yes, yes I know you mean well Sean, but in your profession you cannot be sure that you will be still around, nor me in that case. No, I've been thinking that if I was given the opportunity to make amends, to clear the family name, the girls will be left alone.' She was looking intently at her friend; tears had welled in her eyes.

'You have been thinking haven't you, but believe me, you going to jail is not going to help the girls. People will forget, the girls will be all right.'

'No, you are wrong, and you know it. People round here don't forget, ever. And going to jail – for the cause – would be a Godsend. Heroine of the cause! That would shut the bastards up.'
Bu this time she had tears running down her face. Sean walked across the room and put his arms around her.

'You shouldn't let them be getting at you, you've done nothing wrong.'

'You tell them that.' She sniffled into his shoulder.

'Look, leave it with me, I'll see what I can do.' She looked him in the eyes.

'Thankyou Sean, thankyou.'
She went to give him the usual peck on the cheek but somehow her lips met with his. He responded enthusiastically and they both opened their mouths and became one for a frantic, hungry moment.

They parted slowly. They were both shocked. She was flustered, he seemed frightened. Neither had planned what had happened, it seemed so natural.

'I must be going, things to do.....and that....'

Sean muttered as he made for the door. Katey stood in silence, taking in everything that had been said and done in the last few minutes. For the first time since losing her man she felt alive, vibrant.

—-oooOOOooo—-

'Well that's that done, at the moment we are the only patrol to have volunteered. If we are successful we go across the water in a week.' Andy seemed almost jubilant as he spoke.

'No more Captain Bastard for a few months.' Kev added.

'One last, minor problem. I have gone behind the back of the infamous Captain TS, he'll throw a track when he finds out.' Kev and Steve looked at each other and responded in unison.

'Fuck him.' Everyone laughed.

'That's everything stowed away, anyone coming for a run? Andy invited as he walked back into the crew room. They followed with varying degrees of enthusiasm.

—-oooOOOooo—-

Sean guided the small car through the back streets stopping just round corners and looping through alleyways until he was sure he wasn't being followed. Then he headed towards the Ligoniel horseshoe and the mountain road, out into the countryside. As the steep road approached its summit he turned right, into the old quarry. He didn't have long to wait as within minutes a red Mercedes slowly made its way through the mud to

SCAPEGOAT

join him. The rear window of the Merc drew alongside and was lowered.

'Glorious morning Sean, glorious.'

'Yes Mr Kelly, good to be alive.'

'What have you for me then, good news I hope?'

'Michael tells me the para is ripe for the plucking and that will happen in the next few days. We have found a cottage to let yer man get rid of his drink and get in shape to do the job, and we have confirmed the movements of the target, as best we can.'

'Good, good, I want the para over here by next Monday, tell your brother that!'

'Yes Mr Kelly, that should be no problem.'

'Anything else Sean, me boy?'

'One thing, I was thinking to get a woman to put in the cottage with yer man, it would draw less attention than two men. He isn't going to be a problem.'

Kelly thought for a while.

'Yes, good idea, anyone in mind?'

'The touts wife, McQuire. Give her chance to prove herself?'

'Well we've got a Para, so we might as well have a touts wife.' Kelly was smiling as he spoke.

He raised the window of the Merc as it drove slowly through the mud and turned right onto the tarmac road and out into the countryside. Sean gave it a few moments and turned left, back down the hill, towards the smoking chimneys and dirty back streets.

—-oooOOOooo—-

JAMES RHYS ROBERTS

It had not been a good day for Ralph, he wondered the cold streets for hours. Just after lunch he came across three wino's drinking behind the dole office. They had beckoned to him but he was reluctant to join them. After all these were the same wino's he had criticised, avoided or when necessary, arrested. However, the sight of the cans of high alcohol lager ended his reluctance. He had been told as a rookie copper that every wino had a background, he had been told about the one who had been a teacher, the other who once owned his own factory. They had only one thing in common; a total dependence on alcohol. This bonded them in friendship or at least a comradeship that lasted until they were drunk, when they would usually start fighting amongst themselves. Ralph had arrived at the right time; they had just received their handouts from the social security offices and invested the lot in cans of lager. The newcomer was welcome, at the moment.

'Who are you then?' Asked a large man with no meat on his bones, his ragged, greying beard twisted and matted.

'Ralph's the name, just come up from Nottingham.'

'Nottingham, fine City.' Exclaimed a shorter man, with tattoos visible through his close cropped hair.
They didn't want to know anymore, they had nothing to hide and no secrets. Lager cans were handed round and Ralph started to cheer up.

Michael sat in the study of his house mentally adding the final touches to his plan. Like his younger brother he excelled when confronted with a problem. He stood and went down the stairs to the cellar. He turned on a light and entered a small room that had been completely whitewashed. It had no window or furniture. Empty, except for a plastic bucket and roll of toilet paper in the corner. Michael pulled the large heavy door

SCAPEGOAT

shut with a bang. A small spy hole was situated in the upper centre of the door, and a cat flap type hole at the bottom. He pulled on an overcoat as he walked towards the front door, the Monster sat in the car waiting outside.

It took them only minutes to find Ralph and his new friends, they were still where the Monster had watched them all afternoon. They were now at the arguing stage, 'soon this would turn nasty and they would fight', Michael thought to himself. A taller man walked off, deep in heated conversation with himself. Another two were pushing and shoving each other, Ralph sat ignoring the pair. After a few minutes Ralph seemed to have enough of these antics and staggered off to find somewhere to sleep. He didn't have to search for long. As he stumbled across the ruins of a cutlery factory he tripped and fell. Lacking the strength to get up he slept where he lay.

Michael and the Monster allowed the drunk half an hour to slip into a deep coma before they approached. Michael kicked Ralph in the side and received a grunt in response, he nodded to the big man who picked up the unconscious body with ease and threw it over his shoulder. Once back at the car the body was unceremoniously thrown onto the back seat and the car driven off at high speed. Back at the house Ralph was carried down to the cellar and placed, almost gently, on the floor of the white room. The door was shut; a key turned in the lock was clearly audible, but not heard by a comatose Ralph.

—-oooOOOooo—-

The run had not been particularly testing, the patrol had gossiped their way round the country lanes. The main topic had been the, almost certain, impending tour of Northern Ireland.

The tour would last six months', the patrol would stay together because it was relieving a patrol from another Squadron. The 'phased handover' had become routine following disasters in the early years when a completely new unit had to start from scratch and learn the hard way. As they turned into the drive leading to the camp gates they could see Captain TS in the distance. He was laying in wait.

'Sergeant Woods, a word.'
The Captain commanded as the four attempted to run past him. Andy broke off from the other four who continued on their way.

'Yes, Sir.'
'Good try, but I've discovered your plan of escape.'
'Sir?'
The Captain moved closer to Andy.
'Don't fucking, Sir me. You know exactly what I am on about and I will do everything in my power to block your little holiday across the water, do you hear me?'
'Yes, Sir!' Andy turned and ran away as he spoke.
'That fucking, bastard, fucking, twat!' Andy shouted as he joined the others in the crew room.
'He's trying to block our NI tour.'
The others joined in the verbal hatred of their favourite leader.
'I'm off to see the RSM.'
Andy left the room at a jog and headed for the Kremlin and the RSM's Office. Andy had done selection with the current RSM, and knew he could work wonders for them especially as the RSM couldn't stand Captain TS either.

—-oooOOOooo—-

SCAPEGOAT

Ralph was totally disorientated. His mind was awake, he could sense his predicament and assumed he was back in a Police cell. But, the police would not strip you naked. Slowly he opened his eyes to the blinding light, this was like no police cell he had ever seen, that was for sure. He gradually managed to sit up against the wall. He inspected himself; he hadn't spewed or pissed himself. He looked above his head for the halo he'd seen in the newspaper adverts. A mist occupied the area between his ears, his body ached and his stomach was pure agony. He stood up gingerly and moved slowly over to the corner. With one arm against the wall, supporting his weight, he emptied his bladder into the plastic bucket. He then made his way to the door and hammered on it with the palm of his hand.

'Hello, where am I? Hello!'
He shouted and banged to no avail. He sat down again and drifted gently into a coma.

Sometime later he was woken by the sound of a metal bowl sliding through the cat flap. He crawled over to inspect his gift. Water. He threw the bowl as hard as he could, it hit the wall with a metallic clatter and water sprayed everywhere. Ralph was now cold, wet and thirsty - but not thirsty for water. He set upon the door again, kicking it as he shouted for attention. He was suffering now, the pain in his stomach seemed to be linked directly to his head. He sat down, hunched in a ball, clutching his stomach. The eye at the door checked that all was well.

The Monster went upstairs and reported to Michael.

'Right, put more water in at midday. No words, keep the door closed.'

The Monster, a man of few words anyway, nodded acknowledgement. The banging had started again in the cellar, but neither man paid any attention. As the day wore on the banging and shouting increased but was totally ignored. More water was pushed at intervals through the flap to Ralph only to be kicked or thrown or eventually, ignored.

    Inside the cell Ralph was in a bad way, his mind running riot. When he did fall into a light sleep he suffered nightmares of his family walking into the cell bringing him drinks. In his dream he looked down at the state he was in and tried to hide in a corner. By next morning he was worn out. When the water was pushed through the flap he reached for it and took a deep, much needed drink. He stood up and for the first time since he entered the room he felt he had his senses about him and he didn't attack the door. Michael looked through the spy hole and smiled as he watched him drink.

    Later that day a bowl of thin soup arrived with his usual water. Slowly he sipped at the warm liquid but the pain it caused in the pit of his stomach was unbearable and he had to stop eating. He washed the pain away with the cool water. Common sense triumphed and he tried again to eat, this time he endured the pain and half emptied the bowl.

    An hour later Ralph heard a key turn in the lock and Michael walked into the room closely followed by his large minder.

    'Have you seen yourself, Insurance Man?'
Michael produced a mirror from behind his back; Ralph took a look and immediately looked away in shame. A photograph was then thrown towards Ralph; it landed on the floor next to him, face up.

    'Colour Sergeant Ralph Ellis, Second Battalion The Parachute Regiment, sniper and part time insurance man, is it?'

SCAPEGOAT

Ralph made no reply; in fact he couldn't make head nor tail of the situation. Had the IRA captured him? Was he going to get topped because he was an ex Para or copper? Even to an apprentice wino it made no sense. Michael continued.

'You were in some state when we found you, what do you think you're playing at, eh?'

'I don't know.' Ralph replied, meekly.

'You are lucky, ex Para or not I took a shine to you, I've been where you're going and it's not nice.' Michael crouched down next to Ralph.

'Is that the road you want to go down?'
Ralph shook his head slowly from side to side. Michael put half a dozen photographs in Ralph's hand. Ralph looked slowly through them. Tears welled in his eyes as he saw his children playing in the sand when they were on holiday a few years ago. The tears rolled down his cheeks as he got to a picture of them standing next to him outside the Sergeants Mess, Ralph in full uniform. He looked at the photo and then looked down at himself. Michael stood up.

'I can help you, but you have to want to be helped, and I will want a favour in return. Alternatively I open the front door and you walk away for good. What's it going to be?'
Ralph took another look at the photo.

'Okay, I need help, but I'm not helping you lot of murderers, I'd rather die.'
Michael nodded to the Monster who powered a heavy, swift kick directly into Ralph's face. With a groan Ralph fell backwards as teeth and blood sprayed over the photographs. Michael turned and walked out of the room followed by the Monster, the door slammed behind them.

An hour later more beatings. The Monster used no

weapons, just his hands and feet. Ralph had hardly regained consciousness before the onslaught started all over again. Fighting back was not an option, attempting to adopt the foetal position and hide his face and bollocks was his only choice. As the time wore on the cellar became freezing, Ralph could sense the symptoms of hypothermia setting in. The door opened again, this time the huge man carried a bucket, seconds later Ralph was soaked with ice cold water. It woke him up but the Monster soon put paid to that with another kick full in the face, followed by several to the now unprotected groin.

Time did not exist for Ralph, he drifted in and out of consciousness, and thought he would die. Eventually the door opened and Ralph readied himself for another assault, but it didn't happen. After a minute Ralph opened his eyes to see Michael standing with a large steaming mug in one hand, and more photographs in the other. He started to skim the photos at Ralph, slowly, one after the other. Some landed face down, but some landed directly in front of Ralph's bloodied face. He could clearly see his children, in Wales, at least two of the pictures had their grandmother in them.

'You bastard!' Ralph spat blood as he spoke.

'You have no idea what a bastard I can be. Photo's today, tomorrow you can see your children, in person, piece by piece.' Ralph made an attempt to get up in order to grab his tormentor but the pain proved too much and he fell back to the floor. The door closed again.

Ralph seemed to be left alone for hours. The cold began eating into his body as the pictures burned into his mind. The door opened once more, the Monster entered and soaked him again, this time with hot water. He screamed in agony. The water was probably only warm, but the temperature difference gave the effect of being scalded.

'Surely you cannot be that heartless, your own children.' The voice was Michaels.

'Fuck off!' Ralph managed to reply.

Michael came closer.

'You have one hour. One hour to make up your mind and don't think that we will not carry out our threats. I'm sure you know us better than that.'
The door closed again.

Ralph lay and thought, if it was his life and only his life. But it wasn't. He knew he was caught, but one day, he swore to himself, one day he would take his revenge.

'Okay, you win, I'll do whatever you want. You win!'
He shouted to the walls. There was no reply.

An hour or so later a bowl of hot soup, this time with bread rolls, was pushed through the flap in the door. Ralph sipped at the soup and broke off small morsels of the bread, which he then floated in the soup before eating them. The pain from the cuts in his mouth made him wince as he sipped at the soup, but he knew he had to eat. The room started to warm up gradually. The stomach pains were still there, but the cravings for booze were worse. He could not relax and his mind wandered from childhood to Army, as he walked around the small room sweat covered his face and body. Later the light was turned off, but no one visited him. Lying on the cold floor he tried to sleep, but failed.

Unknown hours later the light came on and the door opened. Ralph strained to open his eyes against the blinding whiteness, but eventually, in the doorway he could make out the shape of Michael's massive colleague. The Monster indicated that he should follow him. With difficulty he managed to stand up and stagger from the room. Up the stairs, along the passageway, turn right, up another set of stairs and Ralph found himself in a bathroom. The bath was full with steaming, foamy water. As he entered, the door shut behind him and he heard a key turn in the lock. He caught sight of a gaunt, haggard stranger in the mirror and realised it was him.

As he soaked in the hot bath the door was unlocked and opened again. The large man reached in and put a pile of new clothes on the floor and finally a pair of white training shoes. The door closed and was locked again. He soaked for another five minutes then got out the bath and emptied the filthy water. On the window sill above the sink he found a razor and shaving foam. He shaved, with difficulty, cutting his chin twice. Finally he scrubbed his teeth until his gums bled. He looked in the mirror, yes, he recognised the man, but the man was ten years older than he had been just a week ago.

He put on the clothes, underwear, a casual tracksuit and tee shirt. The door opened and he followed his minder down stairs toward the smell of breakfast cooking just as he had a few weeks before when he had stayed at Michael's as a seemingly welcome guest. Michael welcomed him into the dining room, again wearing the apron and acting the perfect host. They all sat and ate a huge Irish breakfast, complete with soda bread and potato farls. No reference was made of Ralph's incarceration. Breakfast finished, plates away and they all sat drinking thick, hot, brown tea.

'You are doing well, but don't think for a minute that you've cracked it.'
Ralph nodded at Michael's comments.
'The next few weeks are going to be the problem you have to realise that your addiction is for life. There's no magic cure;

SCAPEGOAT

you will never drink booze again. While you are here you abide by my rules. You do not leave this house, don't bother searching for booze there isn't any.'

'Okay, thanks, but when the job's done, whatever it is, I'm off and my kids are safe, yes?'

'You have my word, you will have money and a new life.' Michael extended his hand; Ralph shook it reluctantly and sealed the agreement.

Michael showed Ralph his new bedroom, it was homely and warm but the artistic wrought ironwork on the window could not disguise the fact that this was just another cell.

'For your own good.' Michael had assured him.
There was a small television and a bookshelf packed with books both old and new. For the rest of the day Ralph lay on the bed and watched the television, he had tried to read but his mind refused to remain focused for more than a few minutes. He still needed a drink, but he now had reason to fight the need.

—-oooOOOooo—-

Sean knocked on the door and could feel the curtains twitching in the neighbouring terraced houses. Katey opened the door, and he could hear the girls arguing somewhere in the background.

'Sean, come in I'll get the kettle on.'

'No, sorry I'm busy. I thought I'd just let you know I sorted that thing out. But you will need someone to look after the girls for a week or so.'

'Thank you Sean, I knew I could rely on you, when will whatever it is happen?'

'Soon, in the next week or so.'

She leant forward and kissed him on the cheek, he turned and disappeared into the evening.

—-oooOOOooo—-

Andy had been back from having a word with the RSM for about an hour when the phone in the crew room rang.

'Sergeant Woods, Captain TS wants to see you, now.' The Squadron clerk obvious had someone standing over him.

'Into the valley of death….' He recited to the rest of the Patrol as he left towards the HQ Office.
He knocked on the door.

'Come in!' Captain TS seemed in a surprisingly good mood. Andy went through the motions of standing to attention, not giving TS the opportunity to have a go at him.

'You've played your joker then Woods, pulled all your favours in.'

'What do you mean, Sir?'

'You know as well as I do, apparently your patrols tour of Northern Ireland is confirmed……….you had better read and sign this years Confidential Report before you leave.'
Andy took the paperwork from the Captain and stood reading. After minute he lowered the report and looked at the Captain.

'You fucking what! *Sergeant Woods has had a disappointing year, displaying professional standards and levels of loyalty much below that expected of an SAS soldier. I strongly suggest his future within Special Forces be reviewed soonest.*' Andy threw the paperwork towards the Captain and leaned forward and placed both hands on the table, face to face with TS.

'One day you bastard I will knock that fucking smug smile off your face. You have crossed the wrong man.'

SCAPEGOAT

He turned and strode from the office almost taking the door off its hinges as he slammed it shut.
   'Woods, you haven't signed your Confidential.'
The Captains words fell on deaf ears.
   Andy told the others what to expect when they were called to sign their reports, they all agreed they couldn't give a toss.
   'One day, one fucking day I'll have that bastard you mark my words.' Andy was ashened with temper.

CHAPTER ELEVEN

   As the days moved on Ralph managed to slip into a routine, the desire to run out and destroy more brain cells began to fade. The words that Michael had spoken were constantly in his mind, he had to face the reality that he would never again be able to take an alcoholic drink. Michael had invited him to take a walk and he had enjoyed the carefree amble through the local park, even if he did feel like a patient with mental problems being escorted. Michael shouted from downstairs.
   'You up there, you having a cuppa?'
   'Yes please.'
 Ralph jumped off the bed and made his way downstairs. The Monster sat in the corner of the dining room, his usual talkative self. Ralph had long since given up trying to make conversation with the huge Neanderthal. Michael entered the room with a tray of teacups and cakes but not a hint of what was to come.
   'Tuck in.' he invited.
Ralph helped himself to a small custard tart and lifted a large cup of tea; he had got his appetite back.
   'You have come a long way in the last couple of days, I think we caught you just in time.'

It was the first time that Michael had mentioned Ralph's condition, it bought him back down to earth.

'Still having the nightmares?'

'Yes, a few, but I'll feel much better when this is all over.' Michael lowered the cup from his lips.

'Have you ever heard of the saying, there's no such thing as a free meal?'

'Yes, just get on with it, what's the job?'

Ralph sensed the atmosphere was becoming serious, the Monster had slipped his right hand inside his jacket.

'Look Michael I am very grateful for what you have done for me and I will repay you in anyway I can to keep my children safe, but don't expect me to love you for all this.'

Michael took a long drink from his cup and stood up.

'The job is imminent, it's across the water. That's all you need to know for now. We're giving you a chance to make a new start in life. Once this task is completed we'll put your bank balance in order, get you somewhere to live and sort out some work.' Michael was walking round the room as he spoke.

'What job?' Ralph wanted more.

'We want you to use your sniping skills, just once one man!'

It was Ralph's turn to take a drink of tea and slow down the proceedings.

'Why me? You have dozens of people, with experience, Christ almighty, you can't be that hard up surely?'

'That's not the point, we want you do the job, you don't need to know why!'

'And if I say no?'

'You know the answer to that, we don't make idle threats, not even against children you should know that by now. You might even enjoy the challenge, the adventure. We would have

SCAPEGOAT

preferred you to have volunteered but have no doubts about it we will not fuck about!'
Ralph finished his tea and stood up.

'How long before I leave?'

'Not long, the next day or so.' Ralph walked from the room and up the stairs to his bedroom. Once there he lay on his bed in deep thought. One side of him actually wanted to do the job, after all he owed Michael, but the other side of him knew that the promised rewards were unrealistic. He was sure that if he survived the hit they, the Provos, would top him, but hopefully not the children.

'No, fuck it, I am not getting involved in this shit, I'll get the kids and look after them.' He said under his breath.

He made his mind up to escape. He could find himself a job. Or even tell the Police of their plan; get him back in favour. The screws securing the wrought ironwork to the window were rounded; he would not be able remove them without tools and a lot of noise. He went into the toilet, locked the door and stood on the closed seat. The small window was unlocked and he believed he could squeeze through it and drop to the ground below, but a closer inspection of the drop cancelled that option. The sheer drop ended with a row of pointed railings that would be difficult to avoid, and if he managed to avoid the metal points he would land in the large rose bush and make more noise than was acceptable. He returned to his bedroom.

—-oooOOOooo—-

'Yes, Ma, I'll only be gone a week or so.....Yes, but she's an old friend, sure you can remember her...yes, I know your memory is going...thanks Ma, the girls will be thrilled.'
Katey replaced the handset and called the girls. 'I have a wee

surprise for you, the bad news is that I have to go away and see an old friend who is ill.' The girls put on their sad faces.

'The good news is that your Nanny is coming to look after you.'
This met with a much better reception, they loved their Nanny and knew they would be spoilt rotten. They ran from the room, noisy and excited. Katey busied herself with sorting out clothes for her unknown task.

—-oooOOOooo—-

The evening meal was a silent affair. Michael cooked and waited on them, as usual. Once over, Ralph made his excuses and went back to his room. He turned on the television, but his mind was elsewhere. The only clothes he had were the one's he was wearing, so he would need a jacket or something. The evening wore on, all was quiet down stairs.

The bedside clock showed two in the morning. The house had been silent for hours. Slowly, and as quietly as possible, Ralph pulled on his training shoes and crept from his room. The house was old and it seemed as if every floorboard creaked under his weight. Gradually he made his way to the stairs, stopping now and then to listen for any reaction. There was none. Once down the stairs he turned left, away from the front door towards the kitchen, he needed a jacket or he would freeze to death. He a planned to leave this house and get back to his own house by hitch hiking or walking, if necessary. Once there he would break in and lay low for a while. He found one of Michael's jackets hanging on the back of the kitchen door, he put it on and made his way back to the front door.

There were bolts top and bottom of the door, he reached

SCAPEGOAT

up and twisted the large metal rod from it's housing. The one at the base was even stiffer, but he eventually managed to unbolt it after getting on his knees in order to apply enough pressure. Only a Yale lock left and he would be free.

The pain was sudden and intense, for a second he tried to overcome it and continue to stand but suddenly there was more pain and he slipped into unconsciousness.

The Monster replaced the Colt pistol in his shoulder holster. It was his chosen weapon, suited his large hands and served as a good, heavy cosh. He picked Ralph up, yet again, and carried him down into the cellar. This time dropping him onto the hard, concrete floor without a second thought. A small dark pool of blood formed on the floor below Ralph's head..

—-oooOOOooo—-

The ringing could only just be heard over the noise of the excited girls playing with their Nanny.

'Shush a while.' Katey shouted as she made her way to the phone.

'Hi, Sean…..yes, I'm ready…ten minutes, OK.'

'Sean? Thought you were going to see a sick friend.'

'Ma, you should know me better than that, Sean is running me to the railway station. It'll save me the taxi fare?'

'Well you be careful in Dublin, it can be rough you know.'

'Rough, Ma. Belfast can be rough Ma. You look after yourself and the girls. I'll ring every day or so.'

'Well let me have your number in case of an emergency.'

'Ma, I told you she hasn't got a phone. I'll be using the one on the corner.'

She picked up her small suitcase and handbag.

'Girls, your Ma's away.'

The girls ran in and badgered their mother for a kiss and cuddle. Katey hugged both of them hard, she had not left their side since they were born. The separation would be difficult but hopefully worthwhile. She could feel herself filling up.

'You both be good for your Nan.'

The girls ran back to their games, Katey blew her mother a kiss and made for the door. Sean was waiting outside, engine running. The curtains opposite flickered as Katey put her case on the backseat and got in beside Sean.

—--oooOOOooo—--

The pounding in his head dragged Ralph from his unconsciousness. For a moment he thought he had weakened and hit the drink again, but no, it didn't feel the same. The light blinded him more than ever. His hand reached instinctively for the core of the pain, the back of his head, it felt wet. He saw the blood on the floor that matched the blood now covering his hand.

'I told you not to fuck us about.'

Michael was standing in a corner, in the opposite corner stood the Monster, pistol in hand. On the walls were large reproductions of the photographs of Ralph's children, they had copied and enlarged the ones shown to him previously of the children playing at their new home in Wales. In the other corner was an unexplained cardboard box. Ralph struggled to sit up.

'You forget, I saved your life. Where do you think you would be now? You were on a one way journey to self destruction, I know - I've been there.' Michael had started to walk slowly round Ralph as he spoke.

SCAPEGOAT

'You are a very lucky man, Ralph. I actually like you, be sure if I didn't you would now be a dead man.'
He nodded to the Monster who immediately swung a boot into Ralph's ribs. Ralph dropped to the floor, his face in the pool of cold blood.

'We mean business, and you will soon realise that if you mess with us once more.'

'I have lived my life with one aim, to give my people a united Ireland. Peace talks or no peace talks I want you fucking Brits out of my Ireland and I will not rest until I achieve my aim.'

Michael was launching into a lecture, Ralph was hovering between listening and unconsciousness.

'You have two choices. One; you do the job. Two; you die and your children go to hell with you.' Ralph was just about ready for the latter.
Michael knelt over Ralph.

' Although I use violence where necessary, I am not a violent man, I am not going to kill you because I don't need to. You will kill yourself.' Ralph tried to raise his head, bemused.

'The box in the corner is full of booze, easy really, we lock you in, we give you booze, booze and more booze. You die, a slow and stupid death.' The Monster kicked Ralph again.

'And when you can raise your head, take a look at your kids, and realise that it could be the last time you see them.' Michael was hovering over Ralph as he spoke, his face inches from his prisoner.

'OK. No more messing about I'll do your dirty work.'
Ralph accepted the inevitable.

—-oooOOOooo—-

JAMES RHYS ROBERTS

Although Katey was quite frightened about the whole affair, she felt comfortable with Sean. They left Belfast by a circuitous route, eventually taking the coast road north pass Larne and round towards Ballycastle. She hadn't been this way since she was a child, memories flooded back as she saw the signposts to this place and that. After Cushendall and before Ballycastle they turned inland and headed through the forest into the Glens. Sean very business like, the kiss not mentioned. As they entered the forest he spoke.

'There'll be a man, a Brit.' He swung the car round a tight bend.

'You don't need to know his name or what he's here for, understand?'

'Yes.'

'You are here to give cover, you are a couple, to the public that is. The cottage we're going to is miles from anywhere, you should have no visitors. You will cook and clean and ask no questions.'

'OK, Sean I've got the message, you can rely on me.'
They turned right up a rocky track. After sometime the track ended in a small yard next to a stone cottage covered in moss and surrounded by bramble. There was a light on inside the cottage and a wisp of smoke coming from the chimneystack.

'Someone came up earlier and lit the fire.' Sean said as he led the way through the front door.

The cottage was old and dirty with cobwebs hanging everywhere. Katey started to mentally jot down a list of jobs she would need to do. Inside the door to the right was the kitchen a long oblong room with a huge deep Belfast sink under the window, flanked on either side by old, scrubbed-wood, draining boards. The left wall was covered with cupboards, above a

SCAPEGOAT

narrow worktop running its length. At the far end was a door that led to an ancient outside toilet and wood store.

To the left, the width of the building, was the living room with windows at both ends. A large log-burning fireplace occupied most of the long wall facing the door, with bookshelves either side. Under the far window was a table and four chairs, the only other furniture a plain old brown settee with matching armchair.

Katey followed Sean upstairs. To the right was a small single bedroom with a narrow bed pushed against the wall. To the left was a primitive bathroom, the once white bath had not been cleaned for sometime. Across the landing to the left was a double bedroom with a large black iron bed.

'That's your room.' Sean blurted out before turning back down the stairs.

'Sean!' He stopped in his tracks.

'Have I done something to offend you?' Katey walked to the top of the stairs.

'No, but this is business. And to be honest I wish I had never got you involved.'

'Don't worry about me Sean, I can look after myself.'

'Right.' Sean gave her long look, but failing to find any words, continued down the stairs, followed closely by Katey.

'I'll be back tomorrow, yer man will most probably arrive the day after, alright?'

'Just one question, Quigley - is he involved in all this?'

'Yes he is, but don't you worry I'll be having a word with him.'

Sean walked towards the car without looking back and drove off. Katey's eyes followed the red of the cars rear lights until they disappeared from view, an owl hooted in the distance; she

149

JAMES RHYS ROBERTS

felt very lonely.

—-oooOOOooo—-

Ralph was back in his bedroom laying on his bed in his mind ran two lines of thought. His initial instinct was that of the hardened paratrooper; not to crack; to find a way to beat the bastards. The other was to drink himself into an early grave and be done with it. Do the job, do it well, and if he got topped at the end of it at least it would be quick, at least the kids would be safe.

—-oooOOOooo—-

Katey had not slept well, she was a City girl born and bred. Every noise from the woods or creak of the floorboards made her sit up in bed. The early morning sun found her drinking tea in the front room. The hot water obviously worked off some kind of back boiler so she carried in logs from the shed and made a roaring fire. While the fire burnt she walked outside with her cup of tea. The yard was bigger than she had imagined in the dark, the paving consisted of large sea boulders set in the dirt. Across from the house were a series of sheds, the largest being the size of a garage, decreasing to the size of a small bike shed. They were in a bad state of repair, jackdaws flying in and out through gaps in the broken roof tiles.

In front of the larger shed was a half-barrel filled with water; next to this stood an old rusty well pump. Katey could imagine an old woman drawing water from the ground, straining to survive. She wondered where the water came from now, but she wasn't too concerned, it looked clean. She went back into the house and tested the temperature of the bath water; it was

SCAPEGOAT

steaming hot so she washed out the big old bath before filling it. Ten minutes later she was in heaven, soaking in deep hot water. She missed the children but she realised that for the first time in years they were not downstairs fighting or banging on the bathroom door demanding her attention

As Sean and Quigley turned up the rocky track, Katey lowered her head under the water, rinsed the shampoo from her long, red hair and surfaced. Quigley walked from the car and into the house, Sean was delayed by the ringing of his mobile phone. Katey stood in the bath and pulled out the plug, towelling her hair roughly as the bath emptied. The sound of the rushing water was music to the ears of Quigley, he guessed what it meant. After glancing behind him to ensure Sean was engrossed in his conversation, he headed quickly for the stairs.

Katey was singing gently, she collected her long wet hair in the towel and rolled in into a makeshift turban. A floorboard creaked, startled she looked up. Quigley stood there, smiling from ear to ear, his eyes running over her full, firm breasts down to her thick red bush.

'Very nice, very fucking nice.'
As he went to walk towards her; she froze, not thinking of covering herself.

'Katey, you there?' Sean shouted from down stairs.
Quigley stopped in his tracks, smiled at her again and closed the bathroom door.

'Aye, she's in the bath. I wish she'd hurry up I want to take a piss!' Quigley made his way back down the stairs. Katey snapped out of her stupor and wrapped a big towel around her body and headed for her bedroom.
Sean came up the stairs and knocked on the bedroom door.
'Did you sleep well Katey?'

'Er, yes.....yes, give me a minute, I'll be down and make you a cuppa.' Sean sensed her discomfort but didn't push the issue and headed down the stairs. Quigley was taking a piss out in the yard, looking up at the bedroom window.

'Tea is it?' Katey asked Sean.
'Two!' Said Quigley, rudely butting in as he re-entered the cottage.
She busied herself with making the tea, aimlessly cleaning the surfaces as the kettle boiled on the rusty cooker.
'He'll be here tomorrow.' Sean said as Quigley took himself on a tour of the cottage.
'Are you going to be alright with this fella here?'
'I'd prefer anyone, to some.' She looked upwards towards the sound of Quigley's footsteps.
'Here's something that might make you feel more secure.' Sean handed her a Walther, handle first. Katey was shocked, paused for a moment, then snatched the gun from him.
'It's got a full magazine, you use it only if you have to OK.' Katey nodded and placed the small pistol in the cutlery drawer to the right of the sink.
The two men left shortly after. Quigley had said nothing, but for the rest of the visit had stared at her body over and over again. Katey was glad when they got back in the car and bounced down the rocky track. Once they were out of sight she had returned to the kitchen and took the Walther from the draw. Expertly she withdrew the magazine and pulled back the slide. She was from the Falls, she knew her weapons. There was no round in the chamber so she replaced the magazine and pulled back the slide. She knew the Walther was unique and showed a round in the chamber by a small protruding metal rod

SCAPEGOAT

above the hammer. She checked this and replaced the weapon at the back of the drawer.

She spent the rest of the day cleaning the cottage from top to bottom. She needed to occupy her mind, she felt dirty, in her minds eye she could see Quigley standing there drooling over her. Later she tried to sleep, but suffered the same dream over and over. In the early hours of the morning she finally drifted off into a deep sleep, only to awake sweating and fighting off an imaginary Quigley, he turned out to be the pillow. Outside the birds began their dawn chorus, the start of another day.

—-oooOOOooo—-

The patrol handed all their team equipment to the stores; they would receive more kit when they arrived in the province. It had been a move at unusually short notice mainly because the outgoing patrol wanted to join their Squadron for a tour of the States. Andy had readily agreed to the quick move in order to get away from his favourite captain.

Unsurprisingly all the others in the Patrol had received mediocre reports from Captain TS, they all agreed, TS would not get away with stabbing them in the back, especially all at once, their time would come. Not an hour went by without Andy expressing his hatred of the man. They finished packing their kit before parting for a long weekend. All except Steve would fly out from Heathrow on a schedule flight. Steve would slog up to Stranraer in his battered old MG roadster and sail on the short ferry crossing. That's if he made it, the others joked.

JAMES RHYS ROBERTS

—-oooOOOooo—-

Ralph was recovering well. The wounds on his head had been dressed, roughly by the Monster and he had been given his breakfast in his room. To use the toilet he had to bang on the door and wait to be allowed out by the huge man who now constantly carried his automatic pistol in his hand. The door opened and the Monster waved his pistol for Ralph to follow him down the stairs.

'Tonight you will leave here and walk into town. My friend here will be with you and make no bones about it, fuck about and he will top you without hesitation. You will be placed in a van and driven to the motorway services. Once there you will be transferred to another vehicle. Throughout the whole journey you will say; nothing. Understand?' Ralph nodded, he would obey the instructions.

'You leave in one hour.'

Ralph returned to his room and was locked in again. A few minutes later huge hands passed in a pile of clothes and a stoat pair of walking boots. Ralph changed, he was now better suited to the outdoors in a thick lumberjack shirt, jumper and jeans. He left the green German parka on the floor for the time being. He sat on the edge of the bed wondering what the hell he had let himself in for.

'Surely I should make one last effort to escape', he thought to himself. But no, thinking of the children he dismissed any idea of a second attempt. Get the job done and out of it all. The Monster arrived and beckoned him to follow. Michael stood in the hall as Ralph followed the Monster out of the front door. No words were spoken.

SCAPEGOAT

It was early evening, cold and getting dark. The tail end of the rush hour was making its way home as both men threaded through alleyway after alleyway. They rounded a corner and were confronted by the open back doors of a small van. Without warning a huge, strong hand grabbed Ralph by the neck and pushed him into the rear of the van. The doors were quickly and quietly closed, the Monster got into the front passenger seat and the van set off.

It was a tight fit in the van as it was full of bags of rubbish. Ralph had to twist and turn to make himself more comfortable. The van left the town and headed up a dual carriageway towards the motorway. At the motorway they headed north for twenty minutes, before pulling into the services and parking between scores of large heavy lorries. With practised efficiency a waiting driver opened the large back doors of his lorry. The van driver in turn opened the van doors and kept watch while the Monster dragged Ralph from the back of the van and threw him into the back of the lorry. The huge man then climbed into the back of the lorry and pointed to a large open wooden box. Ralph got the message and climbed in, arranging his body in the foetal position. The lid was put in place and nailed down, the box was then pushed forward to join other identical boxes. The Monster jumped from the back of the lorry and the driver secured the doors. Two minutes later the vehicles went their separate ways.

Ralph inspected his new, temporary home using the torch he had painfully sat on as he got into the box. He could stretch out a little, but not fully. There were two plastic bottles, one looked like it contained water, the other was empty, obviously for pissing in. As Leeds approached the lorry pulled off the motorway. Half a mile later it reversed up to a loading ramp and another twenty identical wooden boxes were loaded into the back. The driver signed for the boxes, secured the doors and headed north to the ferry port and ferry. Ralph attempted to make himself comfortable, but it was going to be a long, cold journey. As they re-joined the motorway they were overtaken by a small sports car belching smoke. The lorry driver doubted whether the old MG would go much further, but liked to see quality vehicles on the roads now and again.

—-oooOOOooo—-

Katey sat in front of the log fire, she was tired after spending the day cleaning the cottage from top to bottom. Quigley was constantly on her mind, if she thought she heard the sound of a distant engine she ran to the kitchen and took out the Walther, but he didn't arrive. After all the cleaning and her sleepless night she felt exhausted and fell to sleep where she was, the fire was spitting sparks as she picked up her legs and lay out on the settee.

—-oooOOOooo—-

As the night went on and the MG cruised smokily along the motorway, Steve was well aware that he might breakdown. He just hoped he could do some roadside repairs and limp to the ferry. Once on the other side he could get one of the lads to tow him to camp, the engine was going to be totally rebuilt when he got there anyway so minor damage in transit was not a problem. A few hours later he turned left off the motorway and onto the trunk road that followed, roughly, the coastline through the south of Scotland to the ferry port. He stopped

SCAPEGOAT

for petrol and a quick visit to the toilet about an hour out of Stranraer. As he walked back to his car the quiet of the night was shattered by the noise of the lorry he had overtaken earlier. Luckily Steve was not in a rush, and he knew that once you were caught behind a lorry on this road you were stuck there. He was on the tarmac conveyor belt to the sea, only as fast as the slowest lorry.

—-oooOOOooo—-

Ralph had tried to sleep but could not get comfortable, the cold was penetrating to the bone. He began to curse the situation he was in, they might still just top him. The least they could have done was put in a vacuum flask, he banged his head as the lorry took yet another corner. He knew roughly where they were heading and could estimate their progress by the amount of bends they encountered. He estimated they would be at the ferry terminal in about an hour. What then? Would they be in a long queue to load, once aboard he would still be entombed in his coffin until some time on the other side. Well, there wasn't much he could do about it so he concentrated on trying to keep warm by breathing into his shirt and banging his feet. He paused in his exertions for a moment as he realised that for the first time in weeks he had not thought of having a drink, for an hour at least. Sometime later the lorry slowed and took a turn hard to the right. Ralph decided this was the road to Cairnryan, to the northeast of Stranraer. Not long to go.

—-oooOOOooo—-

A few miles behind the lorry the MG loved the winding

roads, Steve dreamed it was a summer's day and that he was driving with the hood down. A couple of times the engine had coughed and spluttered and he thought an impromptu pit stop inevitable but the engine sparked back to life just before grinding to a halt. The lights in the distance belonged to the port so he had made it with time to spare; his ferry didn't leave for nearly three hours. He pulled into the car park and walked over to the terminal for a much-needed coffee, he just hoped the engine would spark back to life just once more.

After coffee he returned to the car and tried to take a nap, only to be roused by an official requesting his ticket and instructing him to follow the other cars aboard. Now was the final test...it started, with difficulty, but it started, coughing out a huge cloud of grey smoke as it did so.

—-oooOOOooo—-

Across the estuary the lorry was loaded onto the ferry almost immediately. Ralph heard the drivers cab door slam as he went for a meal and some sleep. 'Bastard!' Thought Ralph. He could hear other lorries being loaded, the shouting and clanging of chains kept him from dozing off. Eventually he recognised the thump of the large doors of the ferry being closed, then he managed to sleep.

—-oooOOOooo—-

Steve stood on the upper deck as the ferry drew into Larne harbour; already berthing was a transport ferry packed with a load of heavy lorries. He had survived four tours of duty in Ulster, two of those with the Troop. Northern Ireland held

SCAPEGOAT

fond and not so fond memories for him as well as many other soldiers. He had been involved in many skirmishes and had killed when it was needed. But he had also lost comrades, friends whose smiling faces he could clearly see in the dark hills above Larne.

He snapped himself out of his reverie by imagining the severe socialising he would be doing in the next few months, work allowing. The tannoy ordered drivers to their vehicles, he descended to the lower decks for the short journey to join his comrades, (alive and dead).

CHAPTER TWELVE

The movement of the lorry awaked Ralph; the angle indicated that it was leaving the boat. He should have been nervous, what if he was discovered? But no, he half hoped he was found. He would tell them the truth, it wasn't his fault and he had been kidnapped. His hopes and fears were wasted; there would be no shouting they wouldn't hear him anyway. The lorry accelerated from the port car park, he was on his way into the unknown.

The lorry negotiated the roundabout and attacked the hill on route to Belfast. Reaching the top it cruised for some distance before slowing, pulling into the left and drawing to a halt. Ralph heard a couple of different voices, the rear doors were pulled open and the boxes around him were manhandled. Seconds later the point of a steel crowbar appeared violently through the wood above his head, in seconds the wooden lid was ripped off. The rush of air was cold, but welcome. A hand took his arm and he was helped from the wooden crate, initially his legs refused to work and he was forced to lean on the person next to him. Quigley was not impressed and immediately pushed Ralph from the back of the lorry. He landed heavily on his side in the mud.

'Don't you fucking touch me you Brit Bastard!' Shouted Quigley from the back of the lorry as Sean approached from the side.

'What the fuck's going on here, keep your noise down!' Ralph struggled to stand and Sean offered a helping hand.

—-oooOOOooo—-

It was a struggle for the engine in the sports car to get it to the top of the hill, the temperature gauge was well into the red. Once over the hill Steve turned off the engine and freewheeled down the other side in an effort to cool the engine and bring the gauge back down to normal. It didn't work, steam gushed from under the bonnet making it difficult to see the road. He slowed and started to pull over into a lay-by but at the last moment saw that a large lorry and a van occupied most of the room so he kept going. As he continued to freewheel, out of the corner of his eye, he saw movement at the back of the lorry. Someone had fallen and was being helped to his feet, 'probably pissed,' thought Steve. For a moment, he could have sworn he knew the person being helped up. Who? From where? It wouldn't come to mind. Then, without warning, the steam cleared and the engine picked up, perhaps he would make it after all. The half-remembered man went from his mind and he continued his journey to Army HQ at Lisburn.

—-oooOOOooo—-

Ralph was bundled into the back of the waiting van, Sean and Quigley jumped into the front. Sean wasted no time and drove the van back towards Larne. Once in town they turned right onto the coast road. Sometime later they took another right into the forest, and right again up the track to the cottage. The back doors of the van opened, the smell of burning logs pervaded Ralph's nostrils.

'You, stay there.' Sean commanded and turned towards the cottage. Quigley stood guard, revolver in hand. He leant into the van.

'I fucking hate you Brit bastards, and a Para to boot. It would give me great pleasure to blow your fucking brains out.' Quigley took aim at Ralph's head.

'One fucking wrong move, please.' He prayed.

'You, get out the bloody way.' Sean had returned.

'You, out of the van and follow me.'

Ralph got out of the van and followed Sean into the cottage, Quigley followed, the revolver still pointed at the target. They went straight up the stairs and into the small bedroom, once inside Sean closed the door behind them. They looked at each other, Sean gestured for Ralph to sit on the bed.

'Listen and listen well. You are not welcome here, nothing would give us greater pleasure than to put you down like a sick dog. You will not be jailed, you need to train for the task in hand. But try to escape and we will hunt you down, if we fail to find you – we will find your family. The female down stairs will feed you and give you cover. Your story is that you are married, you are here to get over a car accident, hence the training. No names, no conversation, just get the job done and get out of here, understand?'

Ralph nodded.

Sean turned and left the room; Quigley took a step forward and aimed the revolver at Ralph's head once more. This time he theatrically fired the gun, and blew invisible smoke from the barrel before following his colleague from the room. The door was closed but not locked and there were no bars on the windows but the threat to his family had hit home. He concentrated his thoughts, yes, he would get the job done and get the fuck out of here. If he could.

Meanwhile downstairs, Sean was sitting by the fire briefing Katey.

'You'll be alright, a few days and this will be all over and you can get back to the girls.'

'Don't you be worrying about me Sean, I'm a big girl now.' Quigley was raiding the kitchen, dipping a chunk of bread into a stew that was simmering on the stove. He walked into the front room, still chewing the bread as more evidence of his raid ran down his chin. He leered at Katey; she turned her head and stared into the flames of the fire. Sean made towards the door, Quigley followed taking one last look at his future prey before leaving the cottage. The van pulled away into the darkness.

Katey sat for a moment then sprang into action pushing her hatred of Quigley to the back of her mind. She cut two doorstep slices of bread off the large loaf and filled a big bowl with hot stew. Approaching the bedroom door with the tray she became nervous, she knocked and the door opened.

'I thought you would be hungry?'
Ralph took the tray.
'Yes....thankyou....thankyou, very much.'

Back downstairs her mind tried to make sense of it all. 'English, a Brit.... Why?' She had been impressed by her visitor's manners. For all her confusion she felt safer, at least she had company now.

SCAPEGOAT

—-oooOOOooo—-

'The old banger made it then.' Asked Andy.

'Yes, but only just. Had to free wheel almost all the way from the ferry.'

Andy and the rest of the Patrol had arrived on the last flight the night before and hit the bar straight away.

'We've got a briefing in an hour, so grab some scoff while you can.'

'Okay.' Steve replied, he had managed a few hours sleep and was probably in better shape than the others who had fallen out of the bar in the early hours of the morning. After a hearty breakfast in the cookhouse all four made their way across to the briefing room situated in one of the many portacabins. On their arrival they were greeted by the Troop Commander, a Rupert they knew from Hereford, a steady unflappable type. He gave a short introduction outlining both recent operations and future intentions. All in all things were quiet. The PIRA were still into every racket going but the 'peace' was holding and people were getting used to it. The Rupert handed over to the chief spook, a Staff Sergeant from the Intelligence Corps.

'Yes, I can confirm that things are quiet on the surface. But there's something brewing, you will all remember these three.'

The lights were dimmed and a slide projected onto the wall.

'Patrick Kelly. Still at the centre of all things nasty, and his two henchmen; Sean Miller and Seamus Quigley. Kelly now lives on this small back street terrace.'

The slide changed to an aerial shot of the ranch, with horses running in the fields.

'Who said crime doesn't pay'...... the other two are still in

165

the flat on Leeson Street. The bug is still in situ and producing absolutely zilch. Those two hardly talk to each other, never mind discuss PIRA business. All three are still supplying and controlling most of the drugs, porn and protection in the Province. But they are finding life increasingly difficult; the peace does not suit their business. People aren't as scared as they used to be.'
The lights came back on and the Rupert took centre stage.

'They are planning something. We are not sure what but we know it will be big. Source information indicates that they want to restart the troubles. How, we don't know. We do know they were behind the Omagh bomb, but that backfired and cemented public support for the peace. What next? The Det. have been following everything that moves, but we are no further forward. So be ready to move quickly. When it goes down we will need to react immediately. Take the rest of the day to draw and sort out your kit. Test fire your weapons before anything, any questions?'

'No Boss,' they mumbled in unison.

—--oooOOOooo—--

The knock on the door was quiet, almost timid. Ralph was wide-awake and had been for some time. The door opened.
'Here's a cup of tea.' Katey was holding a big white mug.
'I don't know if you want breakfast or anything.' She gave Ralph the mug and picked up the tray from the night before.
'Er, no thanks the tea will be fine.'

Katey turned back to the door, but then stopped.
'I don't know why you are here, in our country, but I'll be

SCAPEGOAT

pleasant to you during your stay. If you want anything just ask, I was told not to talk to you but that won't work, will it?'

'Thanks, don't worry I won't need much; but thanks anyway.' She smiled and left the room. Ralph sat in bed wondering where to start, at least his housemate was friendly and very attractive. He was on the road to recovery; he could tell because parts of his body that had been dead for months were suddenly coming to life. 'It must be angina,' He thought to himself. Or 'Hardening of the arteries.' He rearranged his genitalia as he sipped his tea and smiled to himself.

After drinking half the cup of tea Ralph got out of bed, wrapped a towel around his waist and made for the bathroom. Arranged on a shelf were razor, soap and a pile of clean towels. He ran a bath, took a quick dip, dried and changed into a set of the new clothes. Once dressed he made his way downstairs, Katey was in the kitchen singing, he walked past her and out into the yard. For once it was a nice day, the wispy grey clouds allowed the sun to shine weakly through.

She watched him as he ferreted about in the outbuildings, she was guessing about the whole set up. They hadn't kidnapped him, he was free to wander about and they would have usually tortured and killed him by now. Ralph was rearranging old crates and a rusty old washing machine in the largest of the sheds. He selected a short length of scaffolding pipe from a jumble of rubbish at the back of the building and set about jamming it between two ceiling beams. This done, he tested it by pulling himself up so that his chin met the metal bar. He then placed a plank across two breezeblocks making what looked like a low bench. Katey was intrigued.

Ralph returned to the cottage and went straight to his room. A few minutes later he reappeared wearing a tee shirt in addition to his casual walking trousers and boots. He turned to Katey before he left and said.

'I'll be gone for an hour or two, should anyone be interested.'

'Are you sure you don't want anything to eat?'

'No, thanks.' Ralph replied with a smile then turned and left. Walking left through the yard he followed an overgrown track that led uphill through the forest. He was purposely walking at a quick pace. Within minutes sweat was running down his forehead and he could feel that he was in far from the peak of condition. After a few hundred yards (the he reached the tree line and he broke through to rough open hillside. As he strode out he felt he had a purpose in life, a mission.

He reached the summit of the hill and thought his lungs would explode as he started to cough and retch. Within seconds he was sick, an abrupt reminder of the self abuse of the last few weeks, but he was not going to be beaten, he wiped his mouth and continued the trek. After about a kilometre striding across the windswept hillside he reached a ridge. He stopped and sat on a grassy mound. The view was stunning, The hill fell away toward the sea some distance below and two small hamlets could be seen nestling in the mist. Ralph took long, deep breaths – it was a good day to be alive.

—-oooOOOooo—-

Back at the cottage a car drove into the yard. Sean, on his own. A healthy, happy looking Katey walked out to greet him. Quite naturally she put her arms around his shoulders and gave him a quick kiss on the lips. Sean didn't have chance to respond and was taken aback.

'What a lovely day, I could live here forever.'

SCAPEGOAT

'One thing at a time.' Sean spoke as he walked towards the cottage.

'He's not in.'

'What do you mean; not in.'

'He went out half an hour ago, said he would be an hour or two.'

'Good, for him – at least he's started in the right mood.' Sean continued towards the cottage, Katey followed.

'Tea?'

'Aye, go on then.' Sean replied as he took a seat in the front room. Katey appeared seconds later with two large steaming mugs. They sat in silence for some minutes, both enjoying their cuppa.

'Look, I know I shouldn't ask....but what's a Brit doing here?'

'Yes, you're right – you shouldn't ask.' Sean stood up and took something from his inside pocket.

'Anyway I have a surprise for you.' He handed her a mobile phone.

'We're lucky here the mast is on the hill behind us, press the green button – I've dialled your number in.' Katey was excited, she pressed the button without hesitation.

'Ma, yes it's me, yes, I'm fine. Dublin, yes it's fine, my friend, yes, she's getting better.' Katey paused, shot Sean a big, happy grin. 'Hiya, how you doing, being good for your Nanny. Good. Good.'

Her face became sad, she was missing her children.

'Hiya, your sister says you're being naughty, is that true. No, I didn't think so. Both be good, love you too. Yes Mam a few days, I'll probably ring.'

She looked at Sean for confirmation, he nodded.

'Yeah, I'll ring in a day or so and let you know when I'll be home, see you soon...bye.'

She handed the mobile phone back to Sean.

'Thanks Sean, I really appreciated that, I didn't realise how much I would miss them.'

'No problem, but there's supposed to be no contact, so keep it between ourselves, I'll try and let you have another call in a day or so.'

'Thanks, thanks Sean.' Again she gave him a hug and a quick, thankyou kiss.

They sat and made small talk, finishing the mugs of tea and embarking upon another complete with large slices of freshly cooked fruitcake.

'How's yer man been.'

'Oh, he seems alright, doesn't want anything, doesn't talk much either.'

'Good, keep it that way. Believe me the less you know the better.'

Katey took a mouthful of cake.

'You feel safe with him?'

Katey swallowed her cake and wiped the crumbs from her lip.

'Oh, yes, no problem. It's that bastard Quigley I feel uncomfortable with. The Brits a gentleman compared with him.'

'Well he's been told to stay away from here so you shouldn't have a problem with him, alright?'

'Yeah.' She said as stood up and returned the mugs and plates to the kitchen.

—-oooOOOooo—-

Ralph walked off the hill and back towards the track, breaking slowly into a jog. As he entered the forest he was forced to walk again because of the undergrowth. He was

SCAPEGOAT

sweating like a pig, the tee shirt bore the evidence as a large wet patch on his chest. He walked into the yard and noticed the car, ignored it, and went into the shed. First he started with some step-ups, quietly counting as he used the plank, breeze-block, set up. When he reached a hundred he turned and faced the scaffold bar. He jumped and grasped the bar, hung for a moment, then pulled his body up until his chin touched the bar. After five pull ups he began to suffer. He attempted two more but failed, his chin no where near the bar on the last attempt, so he dropped to the ground and rested.

He could sense he was being watched from the cottage but made a conscious effort not to look in that direction. Removing his shirt he rinsed it out in the barrel of rainwater then dunked his head, wiping the cold water over his face and chest with the tee shirt. He turned and spread the dripping shirt over the scaffold bar and made his way into the cottage and up to his room. Sean followed him.

'I see you've started the work then?' Sean sat on the end of the bed.

'What's it to you?' Ralph replied in an unfriendly manner.

'Easy really, you're not up to doing the job, we get rid of you and get somebody else.'

'I'll do your fucking job.' Ralph was sitting on the floor taking off his boots.

'Tomorrow afternoon we'll be bringing you a rifle, you're to sort it out and make sure it shoots straight.'

'What type of rifle?'

'We've got whatever you want, but we thought a Woodmaster with a good scope will do the business.'

'Woodmaster, good weapon, that should do the trick, I'll see tomorrow.'

Sean made for the door without further ado. Once down the stairs he said his goodbyes to Katey and left.

Katey was busy in the kitchen and waved towards the car as it left the yard, Sean had his business head on again and did not respond. It was ages since she had reason to cook for a man and was enjoying the opportunity. It brought back memories of her early married years when Liam would walk up the street from the factory. She would stand in the bedroom window for an hour waiting for his approach so she could ensure that the meal was on the table for her man. It was the way she had been brought up, look after your man and he will look after you. Her mother had always warned her. 'What he can't get at home, he will find elsewhere'. Things had changed when he got involved in the troubles; he started coming home in the early hours of the morning, if at all. The troubles had changed everyone's life and most people were glad of the peace – but no one voiced their opinion aloud. Not when the likes of Quigley were around.

She finished frying the steak and took the baked potatoes from the hot oven. After placing them on a tray she added the finishing touches of sliced tomatoes and cucumber. She walked up the stairs quite proud of her efforts. The bedroom door was slightly ajar and she could see her guest sitting on the edge of the bed, head in hands. She knocked on the door and coughed gently.

'I have some food for you, but I can keep it warm in the oven if you're not ready.'

'No, come in...thank you.' He accepted the offered tray.

'I'm not sure how much you normally eat, you won't upset me if you leave some.'

'That looks lovely, thank you, I'll try my best.' Ralph cut into one of the potatoes, and noticed that his new landlady had

SCAPEGOAT

made not attempt to leave the room.

'I can't imagine how you, a Brit, has got himself tangled up in this rubbish.'

Ralph swallowed.

'I'm not sure either, but that goes for you too. You don't seem to be the hard faced Provo woman.'

'You've got a point there. This is all new to me.'

Ralph postponed his meal for a moment.

'Belfast girl by the sounds of it?'

'Yes, born and bred – and used to be proud of it.'

'Well I used to be proud of a lot of things, but life goes on and situations change.'

'I've a beer downstairs, would you like a can?'

'No! No, thank you.'

'I'll leave you to your food, shout if you need anything.'

She turned on her heel and left the room. Ralph looked her up and down as she left, he would have liked to have met her in different circumstances that was for sure.

The evening approached, after his meal Ralph had soaked in the bath, changed and came down the stairs carrying the tray. The plate was empty, apart from one untouched baked potato.

'You did well, would you like a cup of tea or something?'

'I wouldn't mind a tea please.'

Ralph wandered into the front room, until now his knowledge of the house had been limited to the door, stairs, bedroom and bathroom. The log fire crackled a warm welcome.

'Is this your place?' He half shouted into the kitchen. Katey came in carrying two mugs of tea.

'No, it's ours. Yours and mine. I arrived a day or so before you did. When this is all over, whatever this is, I'll be away to my wee terrace and my two girls.'

'How old are they?' Ralph was now sat in front of the fire nursing his mug.

'Oh, they're only wee, the oldest, Mary goes up to the big school, in September. Do you have children?

'Yes, a boy and a girl, but I'm separated, I hardly see them now.'

'There's pity, I'm separated as well. Forever. They said my husband was a tout so the heroes of the cause took him away in the night.'
Her voice was becoming intense.

'They couldn't top him for three month's, not until his fingernails had grown back and the burns had healed. They said he made a full confession.'
She stood up and walked into the kitchen, Ralph could sense she was close on tears.

'Thanks for the tea.' He said towards the kitchen as he went back up to his room. There was no reply.

Laying on his bed his mind began to run riot. On his last tour in Belfast, he had been attached to the close observation platoon (COP). They had spent nearly all their tour monitoring the movements of one of the PIRA Quartermasters (QM). Triggering surveillance for the Det who would house the weapons. They had always allowed the arms to move away from the QM before hitting them in that way they could preserve their starting point. 'McQuire!' He thought to himself. Yes that had been his name. The PIRA had lifted him, thought he was a tout. The Army hadn't been bothered, a kill was a kill, even if PIRA had pulled the trigger.

—-oooOOOooo—-

SCAPEGOAT

The evening closed in quickly with a minimum of warning. There was a brief reminder of summer evenings to come as songbirds sounded their call, and then darkness. In the cottage Katey had cleaned the kitchen after the meal and generally tidied up again. She settled in front of the fire and started to read an old classic novel she had found on the once dusty bookshelves. Upstairs Ralph allowed his meal to settle before starting some slow, gentle exercises. Starting with press-ups he progressed onto sit ups and dips, using a chair for support. Initially he wasn't working hard, stopping when he found it difficult, but gradually he built up the tempo alternating the exercises. The beads of sweat began to drip from his chin onto his tee shirt.

Katey could hear the noise from downstairs, but had learnt to keep herself to herself. For nearly two hours Ralph pushed himself to the limit rested and pushed himself again. Eventually he had nothing left to give and collapsed onto the bed, drying his face with a towel as he lay there. His mind was now totally occupied by the task in hand, the threat to his family very much in the forefront of his mind. When this was all over would he sort out a few people? No, if anything this situation had been his salvation, it had stopped the rot. No, if they stuck to their word and gave him the money, he would sort out his life, perhaps get his kids back; or at least get to see them occasionally. But then again, he had to think of who he was dealing with? They wouldn't let him just walk away, they would use him and dispose of him. Or worse still, use him and try to use him again and again. He eventually drifted off into a fitful sleep.

Katey closed the book and placed the last log of the night on the fire. She turned off all the lights and walked wearily up the stairs. As she crossed the landing she saw her guest asleep on his bed. She tiptoed into his room and over to turn off the bedside light. For a moment she paused and looked down at Ralph, she felt sorry for him. Why? She didn't know, but there was something sad about him. She turned off the light and walked quietly from the room, before closing the door she turned.

'Goodnight my little Brit, sleep tight.' She said quietly before pulling the door closed.

—-oooOOOooo—-

The sun in full force brought morning in a glorious manner. Ralph could not remember crawling onto his bed. He felt like closing the curtains to shield himself from the harsh reality of the day. He ached all over, his legs, arms and worst of all his stomach were agony. Had he over done it? No, he thought to himself, time was against him he had to keep up the training, pushing himself as hard as possible. He quickly changed his clothes for trousers and boots, rinsed his face and cleaned his teeth. Once downstairs he started to load his small backpack with bread and cans of soft drink. He found a pasty in a cupboard and some biscuits. It was like being a kid again he thought to himself, off on an adventure. If only. He heard the footsteps behind him and turned sharply.

'It's only me!' Katey stood rubbing the sleep from her eyes.

'You're up early today, come to your senses at last and escaping is it?'

'I wish. No, I'm going off for the morning, be back by lunchtime.'

'Will you be wanting any lunch? Looks like you're off for a picnic.'

SCAPEGOAT

'No, I doubt it, just a cup of your fine tea.'
Ralph turned to leave throwing his backpack over his shoulder. He smiled at Katey as he left and she smiled back. Once in the woods he felt himself coming alive, his aches and pained left him as he powered through the trees. As before he went out of the tree line and up the hill, only this time without stopping to throw up. He felt obliged to again stand and admire to the splendid view of the coastline. Standing for a moment taking in the morning air before turning west and breaking into a jog along the hillside.

Katey meanwhile took a sip from her cup, looked at the clock on the wall and decided to return to bed. The man must be mad she thought to herself.

In the distance Ralph could see two lady hikers standing on the path looking at their map and at the footpath sign. He had seen them early and gradually changed his course to the left, away from them and into a gully. They waved to attract his attention, he waved back but had no intention of assisting. Once out of view he took a long detour to avoid being seen by them again. He had been going strong for about two hours and still felt good but needed to think about making his way back. If he jinked left inland for an hour and left again for an hour or two he should begin to recognise the landscape. He stopped for a moment and emptied a can of lemonade in three gulps. Placing the empty can in his backpack he set off again.

—-oooOOOooo—-

She had enjoyed her lie in. Once awake, she had taken a deep, hot bath and felt like a lady of leisure. No kids under her feet, not a care in the world. But the feeling was short lived as she immediately started to miss the girls. About now they would be in the playground at school, running around and skipping. They were the ones without a care in the world.

She stood at the sink peeling potatoes; she didn't know how many to prepare so she was filling a large pan. In the distance she could hear the sound of an approaching vehicle. Sean no doubt, coming to check that all was well. The thought of him brought a flutter to her stomach, her affection for the quiet, pensive man grew day by day.

A car she hadn't seen before drew into the yard and braked hard. She recognised the driver immediately and a chill travelled the length of her spine. Her grip on the knife in her hand tightened as she saw the face of Quigley smiling at her from the vehicle. Escape was not an option she entertained, she could handle the bastard. Quigley got out of the car and took a large sports grip from the boot, she opened the draw slightly and took a quick, reassuring look at the Walther.

'You're looking particularly stunning this morning.' Said Quigley, putting the grip in one of the empty kitchen cupboards. She made no reply.

'That bag is for your boyfriend, Sean. I was suppose to meet him here but I'm a wee bit early.'

She could sense he was stood close, very close behind her. He stroked her neck, now she was frightened.

'Get your hands off me, Sean will be here any minute.'

'Any minute, maybe, but I'm two hours early.'

He was running his fingers through her hair as he spoke but at the mention of Sean's name he stopped and stepped back. Quigley took a mobile phone from his pocket and it bleeped as he dialled a number.

'How's your lovely girls?'

SCAPEGOAT

She turned.

'Fine, thank you.'

'With your Mother, I believe. Here have a quick word with them.' There was a sinister grin across his face as he handed her the phone.

'Hello, hello..' She hadn't expected an answer, just a wind up by this bastard.

'Yes, yes, I'm here.' A man's voice boomed out, she nearly dropped the phone. What was this all about. The man continued.

'Just a minute I'll get your girls.'
She half turned.

'What is happening, who's got my girls?'

'Mommy, are you there Mommy?'

'Yes darling, don't worry I'm here. Is Nanny there? What man, where are you?

The panic was taking over her thinking, just then she felt Quigley playing with her neck again, this time he was closer, his body against hers. She could clearly feel the hardness of his groin pushing against her buttocks. The threat seemed secondary, her girls were in danger and she was totally helpless.

'Don't cry darling, I'll be home soon to get you. Nasty man, what nasty man, no, he won't hurt you.'
As she spoke she felt Quigley start kissing her neck, she looked down and saw the knife lying there.

'Yes, and how's your sister, I hope you are looking after her.'
His hands were now inching under her arms and starting to cover her breasts, there was urgency in his movements. Without warning he ripped open the blouse, the buttons flying off. She had not put her bra on after her bath, enjoying the

freedom. Her breasts were now fully exposed, his fingers pulling hard at the nipples. He made no effort to be gentle or caring. She made no effort to show pain or resist.

'Put your sister on and stop crying I'll be home soon, yes, I promise.'

His hands left her breasts and her skirt was pulled up from the back. She knew it was hopeless. She could use the Walther or the knife, but kill him and she knew what would happen to her girls. Who had them, who was the nasty man? As she thought she felt her pants being tugged down over her bottom.

'Don't worry darling, I'll sort everything out. Be good, I'm sure the man won't hurt you'

A large boot was kicking her heels apart, reluctantly she parted her legs. Quigley was past caring, revenge was his and it was sweet. He reached down, prepared the way with his dry, hard fingers. Finally and without warning he entered her in a brutal manner. He rammed into her, with her free hand she had to hold onto the edge of the sink.

'No, darling I'm all right, it's just a bad line. You do the talking, I like to hear your voice...' Tears of rage and shame welled in her eyes and her voice shook.

Quigley increased his pace, he reached round with one hand and was gripping her right breast, bruising it with the pressure. His other hand was holding her hips in position for his thrusts. The end was nigh. His face was red and the sweat dripped from his nose, he groaned as he completed the rape. For a second he froze, she could feel his seed entering her body. She felt sick, but couldn't weaken now, she needed to be strong for the girls.

'Alright darling, I'll be in touch and I'll get you out of there soon.'

SCAPEGOAT

Quigley pulled away from her and fastened himself up. Once this was done he snatched the mobile from her.

'Yes, your Mother has been called away, now put the man on. Right, don't forget, touch a hair of those girls and you are a fucking dead man. Twenty-four hours, yes if I don't ring you within twenty-four hours, they're all yours.'
He turned to face Katey, she hadn't moved, her breasts were still exposed. She was in a stupor, mentally trapped. The bastard.

'I think you know the score. The girls are safe, as long as I am.' He walked towards her and picked up the knife from the side.

'So think about the girls before you make any plans.' He pushed the handle of the knife into her hand, wrapping her fingers around it. Grabbing her hand he positioned the point of the blade against his neck.

'Go on, push the blade in. I know you would love to.'
She totally ignored him, he didn't exist.

Ralph felt strong as he ploughed through the undergrowth towards the cottage, on the final stage of his session. As he burst from the tree line he saw the car, he hadn't seen this one before so approached warily. Through the kitchen window he could see the woman with her blank look, staring out onto the yard. He recognised the man talking to her as the bastard he had met when he arrived. The man saw him.

'Put yourself straight woman, your guest is back.'
Quigley tried to close her blouse over her breasts, but she turned and threw him such a look of hatred it made him think twice. She pulled the blouse over her aching breasts and folded her arms to keep the material together.
Ralph walked in, immediately sensing the atmosphere.

181

Something was wrong, but it was nothing to do with him. He made his way to his room without comment.

'I'll be back for some more, and I expect to be entertained. On the bed next time, you'll have to earn your girls safety.'

She said nothing.

He turned with a smile on his face and broke into song as he made his way back to the car.

'I'll tell my ma when I get home, the girls won't leave the boy's alone,
They rough my hair and steal my comb.........'

She didn't move until the sound of the car disappeared into the far distance. All she could think about was her girls. She felt weak, but knew she had to be strong. With one hand she rearranged her underwear, and slowly walked up to her room. Once there she closed the door firmly. Once in the sanctity of her bedroom her brave front crumbled and she collapsed onto the bed and cried pitifully into the pillow. She hated herself for putting her girls in this position, why, why hadn't she just carried on as the Touts Wife. Or better still taken up her sister's invitation to move to Canada. Anything, anything but this.

Across the landing the sound of sobbing stopped Ralph from doing his sit-ups. He knew something was wrong, but still did not feel he could get involved.

Katey reached a decision. In seconds a plan of action formed in her mind reinforced by hatred. She stopped crying, stood up and almost ripped her clothes off – throwing them in a pile. She wrapped a large towel around her body and walked quickly across the landing and locked herself in the bathroom. She drew a deep, very hot bath and lowered herself into the

SCAPEGOAT

scalding water, her skin bloomed into a deep crimson colour but she was oblivious to the pain. Taking a large bar of soap and scrubbing brush from the windowsill she started to cleanse herself from the smell, the liquids of the bastard. It was rape, no...it was worse than rape but the sex act, the filth, faded to insignificance compared to her fear for her daughters. Minutes later she was back in her bedroom, clean clothes, skin raw.

Ralph finished his exercises. The scrubbing sounds from the bathroom had sent a clear message. He was an ex policeman, albeit an officer of the law for only a short period but he knew how most women reacted to rape. Scrub it away, erase it, cleanse yourself. He so much wanted to help, but he didn't know where to start. Get too involved and he would probably get the blame, he would be the obvious suspect. He walked into the bathroom and filled the bath again, looking thoughtfully at the scrubbing brush.

—-oooOOOooo—-

When he had finished his almost cold bath, he dressed and walked down stairs. Katey was sitting by the fire in a trance, she didn't acknowledge his presence.

'I would like to help, I know something is wrong. But it is not my business, tell your friend Sean – he seems a fair man, he'll sort it for you.'
Again she totally ignored him. But she heard him.

Ralph surveyed the kitchen. No lunch prepared, just a pan full of peeled potatoes. He set about attempting to help by making a cup of tea and putting the potatoes onto the stove to boil. There were tins of ham and beans in the cupboard so he placed them on the worktop ready to open. He was no chef.

'Here, have a drink of this it'll help a little.' He passed her the steaming mug, which she accepted.

'Do you want to talk about it?'
She shook her head.

Ralph returned to the kitchen and busied himself with lunch, what he would have done for a microwave. The potatoes came to the boil just as he finished slicing the ham. As he emptied the beans into a smaller pan he managed to drop most of them on the floor. Using a spoon he knelt down and began scooping them into the pan just as Katey came into the kitchen.

'Here, let me do my work.' Katey took the spoon from him. 'And thankyou, but you're right – don't get involved.'

She emptied the beans into the dustbin and cleaned the floor. A new saucepan of beans started to the simmer just as Sean pulled up in the yard. He beamed a smile towards Katey and was puzzled by the blank response. As he walked into the house he shot a glare of suspicion towards Ralph, who stood by the fire.

'Everything alright?' He enquired with total innocence.
She made no reply.

'Hope you've made loads, Quigley should be here in a minute.'

'He's been.' She almost hissed the words as she opened the cupboard and showed Sean the grip.

'He's been, I told him two o'clock – wait till I see him! He wasn't any trouble was he?' He had lowered the volume for the latter enquiry and received a long, long meaningful look from Katey.

'We'll talk after.' He said, almost in a whisper.

Katey put two meals on separate trays and handed one to

each man. She passed a large mug of tea to Sean then, without a word, made her way up to her room. The two men sat and ate in silence. Sean wasn't going to include the Brit in his circle, Katey was nothing to do with him, and Ralph had no intention of swapping notes with the enemy. Both men continued their stubborn silence until the meals were finished, then the silence was broken.

'Let's get on with the business in hand.' Sean said as he walked into the kitchen and returned with the grip, which he placed on the table.

'The Remington Woodmaster rifle. A hunting weapon capable of dropping a stag at four hundred metres and, in the right hands, a man at five hundred.'

Sean began to assemble the rifle, feeding the long metal rod through the wooden butt section and tightening the bolt. Finally he clipped the telescopic sights into position. Ralph sensed immediately that Sean was not a killer. A killer would have instinctively taken aim and looked through the sights at an imaginary target. Just as he did when Sean handed him the rifle.

'You will be given enough ammunition to prepare the weapon, no more. I am sure you realise that putting one of those rounds through my head will not achieve a great deal. The IRA is more than one man.'

Ralph wasn't even paying attention he had work to do. Sean stepped back as the Brit dragged the table over to the window. He then took book after book from their shelves and created a cradle for the rifle to rest on, the barrel pointing up the track away from the yard. Stepping back behind the barrel Ralph aligned the rifle onto a distant target. Once this was done he placed more books about the barrel. Then carefully, without touching the weapon, he looked through the sights.

'Three rounds.'

'Three rounds for what?' Sean was puzzled.

'It will take me three rounds to zero the rifle, but then I'll need a little practice.'

With the point of his dinner knife Ralph started making fine adjustments to the sight. Turning a screw and checking the aim, then repeating the process over and over till he was content with the result. Finally the fine cross hairs in the sight sat exactly on the tip of the broken branch he was aiming at. It was only a rough alignment but would save time.

'Where do I fire it?'

Sean handed him his three rounds, placing each in the palm of his hand as if handing out pocket money.

'Take the path up through the wood, the one you've been using, but turn to the left at the top, yes we have been watching you. About a quarter of a mile along there you will see a gully running up the hillside. A shepherd has left a few swedes about three hundred yards up there, and if you see anyone, don't worry, they'll be our men.'

Ralph closed his hand on the three rounds.

'And to practice?'

'One day at a time, practice day is tomorrow. After you've looked at the ground.'

Ralph wrapped the rifle in a blanket that had been thrown over the back of the settee and made for the door.

'I'll be gone when you return, I'll be here same time tomorrow, be ready to leave.'

Ralph nodded and left the cottage without further comment.

Sean turned to face the stairs and stood for a moment. He had thought it a good idea to involve Katey, not for

SCAPEGOAT

personal gain, not for any of his own reasons. He hadn't wanted, or expected Quigley to enter the equation. What had he done this time, surely he had done enough, he still openly bragged about shooting Liam in the head. Surely that was enough, hopefully he had not told her that they had found out later that Liam was under constant surveillance. No, he's most probably just pissed her off. He set off up the stairs.

The bedroom door was closed, he knocked but got no answer. Slowly he opened the door, at the same time saying 'Katey, are you there...' He heard the sobbing, and knew his excuses had only been just that, excuses for the truth. The stark reality was that Quigley had found a way to hurt her, in some way he had got to, his, strong woman.

'Are you alright?' Came the pathetic question, he knew she wasn't.

'Don't you bother yourself.' She managed to squeeze through the tears.

'What has that bastard been up to, tell me woman?'

'I will never tell you! Ever. The only thing I will tell you is he is a dead man, I will see him in his grave.' She had sat up still sobbing and faced Sean. She looked him in the eye and said in a barely audible whisper.

'Sean...Sean... he's got the girls...'
Sean rushed forward and held her, she grabbed at him as if he were life itself.

'What do you mean he's got the girls? They're with your ma!'

'No! No! NO! Katey was crying more than she was talking.

'He's taken them, given them to some bloke. Another twisted bastard. Sean help me!' She fell on the bed, sobbing. Not another word was spoken, no promises, nothing, just the sound of the car wheels spinning franticly away from the cottage.

CHAPTER THIRTEEN

The patrol went out together. They had a few pints in the mess before getting a lift into the centre of Belfast and starting the serious drinking. Any pretence of being workmen over from the mainland soon went out the window. The 'peace' was in evidence everywhere, there were more women about than ever and the best 'trapping patter' was a pair of gulf war issue desert wellies and the a pager clipped to the belt. As usual the four became too drunk to score but weren't bothered. They rolled out of the pub at midnight singing and holding each other up. Their lift was waiting and once back at camp they carried on the party for another hour.

'I could have scored with that blonde if you hadn't called her a Fenian cow!' Said Andy, tucking into his breakfast as he spoke.

'You couldn't stand, never mind score.' Said Steve in defence of himself.

'I didn't want to stand, she could have carried me home. Anyway, eat up we've got to attend yet another briefing.'

All four finished their breakfast and made their way to the briefing room, they were late and crept in quietly to stand at the back of the room. The Detachment Commander from Belfast continued with his briefing, ignoring the late arrivals.

JAMES RHYS ROBERTS

As commander of one of the army's surveillance units, (known as the Det.), he was responsible for setting up many of the jobs that the SAS had to finish. The captain often likened his task to a game of volleyball. Getting the ball to the net for the 'Regiment' to strike down etc. Unfortunately, as in volleyball, the ball does not always fly where expected and on many occasions they were forced to carry out their own 'strike-down'. They did it professionally and efficiently, much to the annoyance of the Hereford boys as the media would often label such incidents as SAS successes.

'So we are convinced that there is something major bubbling under, the informants know nothing and that in itself is suspicious.'

'Still nothing on the devices?' The Troop Commander enquired.

'Bits, but nothing concrete. One thing for certain is that many believe the peace is going to be short lived.' The Det Officer flicked on the overhead projector as an unseen hand turned the room lights off.

'As from this morning we have placed both Sean Miller and Seamus Quigley under surveillance, if there's something going down they won't be far away. Already we have some sort of result. Quigley!' He pointed at the recent picture being projected onto the screen, 'Was up early and almost certainly picked up a long gun from the hide in the Ballymurphy. Regrettably he was lost heading towards Larne, but there have been no shootings reported as yet. Obviously this is strange in itself; Quigley out of his pit before midday and out of his area. To confirm our suspicions Miller, - he pointed him out - was seen heading towards Larne an hour or so later, but again we lost him. At the moment we have the routes back into the city covered

SCAPEGOAT

for their return.'

'Don't you ever manage to keep your targets?' Asked a familiar voice from the darkness.

'That bastard Thackray-Smith.' Andy half whispered to Steve.

'What's he doing here?'

'Yes we do, as you will no doubt have chance to witness.' Continued the Det Commander with more than an edge of bitterness in his voice.

'But at the moment we would rather let the players run than blow the whole thing before they get chance to set it up!' The lights came back on.

'Any questions?'

'Where do we come into the picture?' Andy looked menacingly at Captain T/S as he spoke.

'As yet we don't know. We cannot forward deploy you because we don't know where it is going to go down, whatever 'it' is. The purpose of this briefing is to prise you out of the sauna and onto immediate standby.' The Officer added with more than a little cattiness.

'Understood.' Replied Andy, acknowledging that the troop had gone into a lax mode over the last few months.

'Any more questions, bearing in mind I haven't got any answers at the moment?' No one replied so the Officer collected his things and left the room throwing a glance of distaste towards Captain T/S. The Troop Commander took the floor.

'Hopefully then you may see some action shortly. So let's make sure we're ready, weapons zeroed, vehicles serviced. We have all got rusty over the past few weeks so let's step up a gear. You all know Captain Thackray-Smith.'

'Gentlemen.' Captain TS took a step forward and introduced himself.

'He is to take over from me in the next few days, much to my surprise I am to be posted to the Jungle Warfare School in Brunei. Typical, I've waited nearly a year for a job like this and now I might miss it, but Brunei is a good second.' The Troop Commander was obviously very pleased about his posting.

Everyone drifted from the briefing room in small groups, cars were revved, and bonnets opened when the release catches could be found among the cobwebs. Several individuals carried their personal armouries to their rooms to clean and oil. Others made for the pipe range. Captain TS caught up with Andy as he made his way to the pipe range.

'Thought you had escaped me, did you?'

'What are you doing here?'

'Just sorting out unfinished business.'

'Well just make sure you don't get in my way!' Andy lifted the HK53 sub machine gun and pointed the muzzle at Capt. TS.

'You never know when an accident is going to happen.'
Captain TS froze in his tracks.

'You are finished Woods, take it from me your days in the Regiment are almost over. I'll see to that.'
Andy walked on without paying any further notice to the Officer.

—-oooOOOooo—-

The engine strained as Sean overtook the lorries heading towards Belfast, caution to the wind as the speedometer needle edged over the one hundred miles per hour marker. It hadn't taken him long to analyse the problem. Quigley was the problem. Quigley was always a problem. He had a good idea where the girls where, well at least who had them. He slowed slightly as he approached the built up area, the grey Audi in the pub car park went unnoticed.

'Standby, standby – that's Bravo One with Alpha One handling towards Green Seven'. The Det surveillance operator eased his car out in pursuit of Sean.

With a screech of tyres Sean arrived at the Club and left the car at the kerb, engine running. The hood on the door attempted to swap pleasantries but was brushed aside. In the late afternoon the club was almost empty, except for a few who virtually lived there. Sean pointed a finger at one and indicated that he should follow him out to the toilets, his command was obeyed. Once in the stinking latrine Sean kicked open the only cubicle to check they were alone. The man had not seen him in a temper like this before, Sean was always the quiet thinker.

'Sean, what's the problem?'
Sean turned, pistol in hand.
'Quigley has been up to something, you have ten seconds to tell me what you know.' The pistol was now levelled at the man's head.
'Sean..Sean...It's me. I'll tell you anything you want to know'.
'What's Quigley been up to, where's he been and whose he been talking to?'
'Look Sean, we haven't seen him for two day's. He took Jimmy off on a job, but he didn't tell us anything; honest.'
Sean lowered the gun.
'Look I need to know, get about – don't let Quigley know. I need to know where that weasel Jimmy is, understand?'
'Yes, course Sean – you can rely on us. Don't worry we'll

find him.'

Sean was walking away before the man finished his promise.

'Alpha One from the Club and complete Bravo One and mobile left.' The Operator on the motorcycle pulled out from the alleyway.

Sean knocked as he opened Katey's front door. Her mother came in from the kitchen.

'What in heavens name is happening Sean? Who were those men?'

'What did they look like Ma?' He tried to act calm, but was failing.

'The one, I've seen him with you, a ginger man, but the other; I haven't seen him before.'

Running around like a headless chicken was pointless, Sean knew that, so he accepted the offer of a cup of tea. Any approach to Quigley was out of the question, evil bastard that he was, anything could happen. They made small talk; he told her the girls were safe, that there had been a misunderstanding. Ma was getting old; she clutched her cup nervously, ignoring most of what was being said.

'Standby, standby – that's A1 from the house and complete Bravo One and mobile.'

Sean drove off deep in thought, forgetting his usual vigilance and totally unaware that he had a five-man surveillance team following his every move. He had an awkward act to balance, the job was to go ahead in two days time. Kelly would except no excuses.

CHAPTER FOURTEEN

Ralph made his way through the woods towards the hillside. The rifle slung over his shoulder was covered with strips of sacking so that from a distance a passer by would be unable to identify it for what it was. Turning right into the gully he immediately saw the vegetable targets. He selected a firing point on a slight mound rising above the fern and lay down in a firing position. The bolt clicked and clunked as he fed a round into the chamber. Carefully he looked through the telescopic sight and placed the crossed hairs on a swede. Steadying his breathing he took the first pressure on the trigger. As he slowly exhaled he completed the pressure and sent the round towards its target. Still looking through the sight he saw the earth jump, slightly to the right of the target. He pulled a screwdriver from his pocket and made a slight adjustment to the sight. Another shot and a small piece of vegetable flew into the air, another adjustment. The last round and a direct hit, smack in the centre. Ralph took a final moment to make sure the locking screws were secure on the sight, picked up the empty cases and placed them in his pocket. Once he was happy that any evidence had been removed from the scene he made his way back to the cottage.

JAMES RHYS ROBERTS

As he walked down the hill he felt confused. On one hand he felt that he again had a mission, an aim in life, but on the other he found it impossible to focus on the main problems. Would he really murder a man for the IRA? Were they going to let him live, were his family safe or would they really carry out their vicious threat if he failed? These thoughts swam his mind, he found it impossible to forge a distinct decision; impossible to reach a conclusion. Ralph stopped and watched as a kestrel hovered over the hillside, one of the beauties of the natural world, busy searching for food for his young family secreted away in an old crow's nest deep in the forest. As he watched it swooped, then aborted the effort and flew away over the crest of the hill and out of sight.

Pushing his way through the trees he wondered about the problems of his temporary landlady. The ginger bastard had obviously upset her. Rape was an upset in the worse possible way, but why should he become involved? Once in the yard he placed the rifle in the hiding place he had prepared, high in the beams of the barn. There was no sign of life in the cottage, so he put the kettle on, filled two of the large mugs with tea and went up the stairs with one of them, walking heavily to announce his presence. He received no answer when he knocked on the bedroom door so he quietly turned the handle and pushed the door open. Katey lay on the bed, face pushed deep into the pillows.

'I thought you might like a cuppa?'
A red, swollen eye appeared.

'Thank you.' The face disappeared back into the sanctuary of the pillow.

'If there's anything I can do to help, just talk perhaps?'
The face appeared again. Not the pretty, healthy face from

yesterday. But a tear stained, swollen-eyed face, suffering, but proud.

'And why should you be bothered, it's not your problem. After tomorrow you'll be on your way, I have to live with this shite!'

'No you don't, get out of it. Move to the mainland, go abroad, you don't owe these bastards anything.'

'What do you know? Nothing, that's what. I'm the Touts Wife; I will live my life paying for my man's disloyalty. Never to be forgiven.'

Ralph moved forward and sat on the edge of the bed; she was surprised and sat up to face him.

'You're no Touts Wife and you know it. Your Husband, Liam I recall, was one of the most dedicated PIRA men in Belfast. My Unit worked against him for month's, he was good, but we could have arrested him at anytime.'

He had her full attention.

'So, why didn't you?'

'Because the Special Branch don't work that way. He was the start point, if a job was going down we would follow your husband, one way or another he would be involved.'

'But how did you find out about him, he always covered his tracks.'

'A Tout, a real Tout. I don't know who, we never did, but I clearly remember the initial information came from an informant close to Liam.'

She sat in silence, in deep thought. Only half a dozen people knew Liam's involvement, they always worked that way. Ralph stood up and made to leave the room.

'I don't know who you are, or why you are being kind to me, but after the job I wish you luck. I am getting a feeling I know what you are here for – doing other peoples dirty work. You should be hitting the parasites, the Kelly's of this world.'

'Kelly, not Patrick Kelly, is he's still running about?'

'No, not running about, running the show. All the drugs, the whores, you, me and all things illegal. People like him can't survive without the 'Troubles'. You should have him in your sights, you would be doing mankind a huge service.'

It was Ralph's turn to pause for thought.

'I'll bear that in mind.' He turned and went back down the stairs to his tea.

—-oooOOOooo—-

Sean had purposely kept a low profile and did his waiting at the flat, Quigley was nowhere to be seen. The mobile phone lay on the cheap, plastic, kitchen tablecloth, which was still covered with the remains of Quigley's supper from the previous night. The phone rang, Sean answered it before the second ring.

'The Ballymurphy, Jimmy was seen there this morning buying bread and bits from the corner shop.'

'Good, good work.' Sean replied.

The caller was standing in the remains of a phone booth near the shop.

'We'll ask about, and cover the shop, he'll be back and we'll follow him to his hidey hole.'

Sean almost managed a smile, they were half way there, he just hoped the girls were safe. He wouldn't be racing up to the Murph, he would be spotted in minutes, his face was too well known. He rang Katey but played down the news in case the outcome was not the one they wanted, she sounded less hysterical.

'No sign of Quigley then?' Not hysterical but still

SCAPEGOAT

frightened.

'Kelly's got him running about, you'll not see him till the day after tomorrow.'

'When are you coming back here Sean?'

'Tomorrow, I'll be there mid morning to take yer man to look at the job. But don't worry I'll keep tabs on Quigley and if he slips away you phone me straight away I'll sort that bastard out.'

'But the girls Sean, we can't do anything till we find my babies.'

'Don't worry, you heard Quigley. The creep won't dare go near the girls till Quigley gives the word, by which time the girls will be safe and sound.'

'Okay goodnight Sean.'

'Goodnight.'

—--oooOOOooo—--

There was an air of expectancy in the briefing room, the usual laughter was subdued. The Standby Patrol had taken to wearing their boots and combats constantly, their tracksuits put away for the time being. Each of the four patrols sat in their own grouping, Captain TS sat on his own at the front. The chief spook entered the room accompanied by one of the Branch Sergeants.

'Gentlemen, things are shaping up.' The Spook turned and pulled back the curtains covering the briefing board.

'The Det picked up Miller speeding back to Belfast from the north Antrim coast area. He was not the usual 'hyper aware' Sean that we have grown used to. He was followed to the Club, the McQuire woman's house and onto his flat. The woman is not at home, according to one of the sources she has left her children with her mother, which is very much out of character. The device at the flat picked up Miller on the mobile to a female, almost certainly McQuire. The day after tomorrow; Saturday, seems to be significant. But why, we don't know.'

'Any sign of Quigley?' Andy enquired.

'Surprisingly; no. As you are all aware they usually work hand in hand. There has also been mention of another man – an unknown.'

The Special Branch man came to his feet.

'At the moment we have an area, albeit a large one, irregular behaviour, a woman and possibly a day. What we now need is the target and the identity of the unknown man. He is thought to be an outsider, someone from the South or even the States.'

'Surely they have got dozens of men available to do a job?' Captain TS stamped his card in the question game.

'Yes, dozens, if not tens of dozens. But we've been expecting something like this, they've continually tried to destabilise the Peace. The criminal element of both the Loyalists and PIRA are thought to be working in league to secure their survival. Blast bombs every night, even the 'Rah' supplying commercial explosives for the Loyalists to do the "up and under" on the woman's car the other week. They all want a spectacular, they want the troubles back – but they don't want the blame.'

'And it could take any form?' The Spook added.

'Yes, any form – a big bomb was tried but failed. We intercepted that in Hillsborough before it even got into the City. So they could try a shoot or whatever. But the target will be either big or important. We don't think it will be a bomb, as they would have to prepare another one and know they have a leak in their ranks. So that leaves a shoot, one man to pull the trigger – an unknown. One target, an important target. One whose death would cause uproar. We have our ideas and we are warning off any possible targets. But the powers to be, whatever the outcome, want the PIRA activity to have no effect on the Peace Talks.'

'We can't give bodyguards to every politician, senior policeman or VIP in the north Antrim area, there must be hundreds.' Captain TS couldn't get his brain to accept the concept.

'I agree, but that's not the plan. We will, if possible intercept the job before it happens. If that happens we would not want any prisoners to complicate the issue and give unnecessary publicity. If they succeed in their mission we will hound them into the ground, we will also take every step to hide their success, it will not have happened. What that means at this stage, and what steps it will require, we don't know but as you can appreciate this will not be your usual operation.'

The meeting broke up and the various groups wandered off. Andy took his patrol for a brew. Socialising and drinking had moved into the background; the importance of the task in hand was paramount and occupied the thoughts of everyone. This was what they had joined the Regiment for, all the training and all the effort. Andy put the kettle on and opened his locker taking out the makings.

'All for coffee?' Andy was filling the mugs as he spoke, no one objected.

'Cheers.' Bob accepted his mug.

'Do you want this or not.' Andy offered the mug to Steve.

'Seen a ghost or something?'

'That photo on your locker. Your mate, the copper.'

'What about him?' Andy took a seat.

'Is he still a copper, on the mainland that is?'

'I don't know, why you missing him?'

Steve sat quietly his gaze still glued to the picture, the coffee dripped from his cup onto the carpet.

'Steve man, snap out of it, what's the problem?'

Steve placed the mug on the floor and walked over to the locker. Carefully he pulled the photograph from the inside of the door.

'It's him, I'm sure.'

'It's fucking who?' Andy stood up and joined him looking at the photo.

'When I drove over I saw him at the back of a lorry, I thought he was pissed but it didn't seem right. At the time I was more interested in making it to camp, the engine was playing up. But, yes….yes, I'm bloody certain it was him, he's over here.'

CHAPTER FIFTEEN

Sean woke early at the flat. The snoring from the neighbouring room confirmed that Quigley was still in residence. He had staggered into the flat in the early hours with some tart in tow, Sean had been tempted to beat the truth out of him there and then. Sense had prevailed and Sean had spent the night suffering the sounds of his colleague and his young lady exercising their animal instincts till dawn approached.

Friday was another bright spring day, Sean left the flat and turned immediately up an alleyway, ignoring his parked car.

'A1 foxtrot left of Charlie One, and left again up the foxtrot option and unsighted.'

Sean knew the importance of the day's activity, the slackness of yesterday was history and he was the professional terrorist again. Before reaching the end of the alleyway he opened a back gate and walked into the kitchen of a house, closing the back door behind him. He sat at the small table and helped himself to a cup of tea from the hot teapot.

'No sign of A1 at the top of the alley, checking the main road.'

'Roger that, all callsigns be aware that A1 is possibly running free, check all options.'
Several cars and two motorbikes tried to keep their speed down as they frantically searched for Sean. Over twenty minutes passed and the search circle grew, to no avail.
'All callsigns, A1 has either escaped or gone to ground, continue to stakeout the area.'

The milkman made his way up the street stopping every five yards or so to place full bottles on doorsteps and fill his crate with the empties. As he placed the two fresh bottles onto the doorstep he noticed the front door open slightly, he knew the drill, he'd done it before, he pushed the door open and disappeared briefly from view. Seconds later the milkman reappeared, the white coat appeared a little large this time because the figure was slightly shorter. Sean placed the empties on the back of the float before jumping behind the wheel and driving out of the street. Several streets later he took off the coat and threw it into a dustbin before driving off in a vehicle that had been parked with the keys in the ignition. Pulling a flat cap on his head and placing a pair of black framed glasses on the bridge of his nose he drove the car into the early morning traffic, passing a stranger sitting in a small builders van.

'All Callsigns return to base, he's either gone to ground or escaped.'

The builder's van moved off out of the city as Sean turned right up Springfield Road towards the Ballymurphy estate. Turning off the main road he parked neatly between two large vans. Within seconds he was making his way on foot

SCAPEGOAT

through the back alleyways. He noticed movement behind the upstairs net curtain as he approached the back door of the dilapidated flats, the door opened before he had chance to knock.

'No sign of him I take it?'

'No Sean, sorry, but don't worry he'll show. He'll need baccy soon, if not food. We have a good view of the shop fronts and Brendan here is ready to tuck in behind him when he starts to return to his lair.'

Sean relaxed slightly, 'How's the family Brendan son?'

'They're good, thankyou. And don't worry Sean I have daughters remember, we'll get the bastard.'

'Well I'll be off then, but remember I need a quick result. Ring me on the mobile the minute you have an address.

'No problem Sean, No problem.' The man replied without taking his eyes from the window.

Sean made his way back to his vehicle, then out of Belfast over the mountain, the long way but the safe way. Once into the countryside he reached into his pocket and dialled Quigley, he got through after two attempts.

'It's me, don't be leaving the City today there's peelers everywhere. Yes...but I've got to recce the job remember. We'll meet tonight to go over the job. Yeah, you too.'

He hung up and threw the phone onto the passenger seat as if he hated it. He only hoped now that his warning had not been too obvious; an unfounded worry as Quigley was busy rolling over onto last night's scrubber for sloppy seconds. The Touts wife could wait till tomorrow.

—-oooOOOooo—-

'You bloody well lost him!' Captain TS was pacing round the Control Room.

'Surveillance is not an exact science you know.' The Det Commander was defending his Operators efforts.

'Miller has been at this game longer than you have been in the Army.' His patience with TS was wearing thin, rapidly. The Chief Spook attempted to pour oil on the troubled waters.

'We have all the main roads to the Antrim coast covered, it's only a matter of time before he shows himself, he's not invisible.'

Back in the basher Andy had convened an extraordinary meeting of his patrol. A quick phone call to the mainland had confirmed that Ralph had left the Police, and apparently his family.

'Can I count on your backing then, as I've said Ralph would not get involved in anything like this willingly. He's on our side, so we'll talk first and shoot later, agreed?'

'You can count on us.' Bob replied on behalf of all the Patrol.

—-oooOOOooo—-

Sean had planned his route well, keeping to back roads for the whole journey. Not once had he spotted a Police patrol, uniformed or covert. There seemed to be more helicopters in the sky than usual, but this did not concern him in his anonymous vehicle. He turned onto the track to the cottage and stopped for a minute or so to check for a tail before continuing to his destination. As he drew to a halt Katey walked towards him with a welcoming but nervous smile on her face. She looked around, confirming that Quigley was not present, only then did she relax and give Sean a kiss. Sean responded holding her close. Sean noticed Ralph standing in the doorway and pushed Katey gently away, making no attempt to hide his affection for her.

'You ready to go then?' Sean held his stare at Ralph for a deliberate moment.

Ralph nodded and walked towards the car. It was more than just a journey, it was the point of no return. Commitment from Ralph. Sean sensed the Brit meant business. No further words were spoken as both men got into the car. Sean did a quick three-point turn and looking at Katey as he drove away. Katey stood and watched feeling vulnerable again as she was left on her own. Once the car was out of sight she went back inside the cottage, straight into the kitchen. Once there she retrieved the Walther from it's hiding place and checked it over, just for reassurance. She hid it again and busied herself, making a meal for the two men to eat on their return.

The two men continued their bumpy and silent journey, Sean had spent many hours rehearsing the circuitous route to the river. Ralph concentrated on taking in his surroundings in case he needed the knowledge in the next day or so. Now and again they caught the odd glimpse of the sea to the north, but for most of the journey high hills or forestry surrounded them. Ralph noticed that as they started to go south the barren landscape turned into well cared for farmland. Sean pulled the car into the gateway of a wood.

'This is your drop off point for tomorrow and should anything go wrong this is where you head for, understand?' Ralph just nodded.

Sean got out of the vehicle and Ralph followed him.

'The river is through the wood and down in the dip beyond, if you have any questions now's the time to ask them.' Sean locked the car and walked off briskly into the wood, Ralph again followed.

The wood consisted mainly of large, mature conifers. The ground was clear but the branches of the trees whipped hard into the faces of the two men as they pushed on, after ten minutes or so Sean stopped.

'We're nearing the edge of the wood', he whispered. 'Very quiet now, we'll move to the fence and have a look at the grounds.'

Sean nodded acknowledgment, and followed Sean at the new, more cautious pace.

As they progressed Sean moved onto his knees, Ralph followed suit. A fence appeared ahead and Sean got down on his belly and moved slowly up to it. Ralph pushed in beside him.

Before the two men was a wide-open valley of lush green moon grass, on the higher ground were the scars of years of peat digging. A river of medium width, approximately thirty feet across, filled the valley floor. The river was in full flow the brown peaty water showing white as it hit the huge rocks. The banks housed several large clumps of gorse that were beginning to flower yellow. They offered the only cover apart from the wood they were currently looking from. Sean whispered again.

'There is a footbridge up to the left about four hundred yards and the big house is about a quarter of a mile upstream. There will be security, at least two armed bodyguards, you'll only get one chance. The main man should be fishing his way down, he has done for the last forty years so there's no reason

SCAPEGOAT

he won't do the same tomorrow. Any questions?'

'What weapons will the security have?'

'Automatic pistols mainly, but they have been known to carry a long gun.'

'Pick up? How far have I got to go?'

'Not far, I'll show you on the way out.' Sean started the return journey still on his stomach. Ralph did not immediately follow, taking time to study the ground in front of him.

Ralph slowly stood up to get a better view of the valley; using the trees as cover he scanned the killing ground. He had done a bit of salmon fishing himself in Wales and could identify with the quality of the water. To his left the river narrowed and fell in a small waterfall. The water below this was deep and slow, an ideal holding area for tired salmon. To fish this small pool the fisherman would position himself at the neck, just below an outcrop of rock, unsighted to Ralph from the tree line. This meant breaking cover and positioning himself somewhere in the gorse to his front, not ideal as it was an obvious and easy place to identify as well as difficult to escape from across open ground. He searched for an alternative but could see none. He lowered to the ground and crawled back towards Sean who was waiting in the wood, they both came to their feet and walked deeper into the trees, taking a slightly different route back. After ten minutes or so they came across a muddy forestry track. Sean halted.

'Up there, about three hundred yards is your pick up. If you haven't done the job don't bother going there. Quigley will be there with a car and there will be a youth on a motorcycle. You hand the rifle to the youth and you get into the car, understand?' Ralph nodded.

'From there?'

'You will find out then, one step at a time.'
'Is there another step?'
'Yes, there is another step, I promise you.'
Sean turned into the trees and headed off to where they had left the car, Ralph followed deep in thought, 'last step, yes, he could imagine where he was going to end up. He could imagine the orders Quigley had been given.'

—-oooOOOooo—-

Andy walked into the portacabin and closed the door behind him. 'They've got Quigley in the flat with some tart, Miller is loose, and fuck knows where my mate Ralph is!' The Patrol was sat waiting for guidance.

'Come and have a brew, we know the area. No doubt we will be moved there shortly, Quigley is a donkey, he will lead the Det to the job.' Bob was almost casual in his summing up of the situation.

'I suppose you are right, but we must make sure we are in at the crucial moment and that bastard TS is nowhere to be seen.'

'He will be chained to the Ops room, like a good Rupert should be.' Steve added, with more than a little contempt.

—-oooOOOooo—-

The mobile phone rang and rang, stopped, started and rang again. Eventually the quilt was thrown aside and the pale, sweaty frame of Quigley moved drunkenly and picked up the noisy item.

'Yes!' Quigley demanded. 'Sorry, sorry Mr Kelly, yes I was

SCAPEGOAT

in the shower, yes.'

Patrick Kelly was in his stables having just taken one of his morning rides along the banks of the Lough, he was sweating, the horse was frothing from the mouth. He treated animals like he treated people, with total disregard for their well being. In fact he treated people like animals with the same rational.

'Listen Quigley and listen good, tomorrow, you know, tomorrow?'

'Yes Boss, I'm not thick yer know!'

'Okay, after the job you pick yer man up, he's to go nowhere but to see his maker. There'll be no motorbike, you're to leave the rifle by his side, don't be fucking touching it, or him, no prints. Once it's over you get straight back to the cottage, and give the touts wife the same treatment, you understand?'

'The woman, come on Boss she's no problem.'

'You just carry out orders, she won't be a problem if you deal with it - right?'

The naked tart walked past Quigley as he replied.

'Okay Boss understood, you can rely on me.'

His words were wasted, the Boss had hung up.

—-oooOOOooo—-

Technology was catching up but the switch to the digital system on mobile phones still posed a problem for the Army monitors. Efforts to get a listening device into Kelly's place had been unsuccessful they only had the intelligence from the flat to work on. ' The woman and Okay Boss understood, you can rely on me.' It wasn't much but it confirmed something was afoot, Quigley was never that polite to anyone. Whatever it was, it was imminent and important.

—-oooOOOooo—-

It was ten o'clock. All and sundry had been summoned to HQ at Lisburn. The Commander Land Forces sat patiently as he listened to the briefing. The small man in the checked jacket next to him constantly whispered into his ear. The man from London rarely spoke aloud; directing all his comments via the General.

'So we are convinced something is going down in the next day or so?' The General was not addressing anyone in particular so Captain TS jumped at the chance to show his presence.

'Yes Sir. Probably sooner than later.'
The checked jacket whispered again to the General.

'And on what do you base that opinion Captain Thackeray-Smith?'

'Er, well Sir, just the activity that has been observed, all the pointers are……well, we think it is imminent.'

'Very informative; can someone put the meat on the bones for us?'

'Yes Sir.' The Det Commander took centre stage.

'Sir, we know the area, Kelly is behind it, Miller is running it and Quigley is involved. There is an unknown element; a third party, possibly a mercenary.'

'And the aim, Simon?'

'To get the troubles up and running again Sir. Peace is no good for the likes of Kelly.'
Another whisper from the jacket and the General stood up and faced the assembled audience.

'Gentleman, you could be right, or wrong, whichever we

SCAPEGOAT

cannot afford to sit on our arses and mop up after these pond life. Deploy your troops with the aim of intercepting this action and failing that they are to react immediately and deal with all those involved.'

'And arrests Sir?' Captain TS tried to get involved again.

'We have a yellow card Captain, I'm sure your troops can use their initiative, even if you can't. I want it clean, no come backs.'

The General's entourage swept from the room. Captain TS regretted his attempts to show the General that he was at the helm of the Special Forces efforts.

—-oooOOOooo—-

The flat in the Ballymurphy was becoming smelly and boring. The atmosphere tense, the girls huddled together under a coat, comforting each other. Across the room Jimmy was unshaven and if he had bothered, could have smelled himself. He was getting more on edge by the minute, down to his last few cigarettes and not having had a call from Quigley was becoming all too much for the pervert. The curtains were shut tight and the television turned down low, the girls tried to avoid the evil stares of their captor. Being Saturday morning cartoons and children's programmes started on the television that at least occupied the girls, allowing them to escape from their situation for a moment.

CHAPTER SIXTEEN

In the big house by the river the ageing angler selected his rod for the day before joining his son for a hearty breakfast.

'Looking forward to the days sport?'

'Sport, yes, I suppose I am. But I can't see it being very fruitful what with the factory ships chasing the fish across the oceans. The nets on the estuary, the poachers and finally me and my little rod. I feel almost guilty for attacking the wee beasts.' Lamented the man who had made similar statements every year for as long as his son could recall.

'Don't forget the security threat, they seem serious with this one.'

'Aren't they always. One threat or another, if we listened to them all we would never get out of the house. But I'll take both the boys and get them to bring the rifle.'

'I'll be away till tonight, meeting at the Orange Hall in the City.' The younger man stood and made to leave as he spoke. 'You have a good day and catch us a big 'un for our supper.'

'Aye I will, and you don't forget, don't weaken, no surrender of weapons, no ceasefire.' The older man raised his voice almost to its old level.

JAMES RHYS ROBERTS

'No Surrender!' He son proclaimed as he left the room.

—-oooOOOooo—-

As Ralph lay awake in bed the sunshine burnt through he windows. He could hear activity below him in the kitchen but was reluctant to rise until invited, he didn't want to be in the way. There was a quiet tapping on the door then it opened slowly, his landlady smiled as she entered carrying a breakfast tray. Ralph sat up and accepted the tray with his usual smile, 'breakfast for the condemned man', he thought to himself.

'I sense today is the day.' She spoke quietly. Ralph nodded acknowledging her intuition.

'I just like to say, well for a Brit you're not a bad man. I felt safer with you than I did with some of my own country folk. I wish you well for today, may you get back to your own, safely and soon.' With a warm smile she turned and left the room. Ralph drank slowly and thoughtfully from the large steaming mug of tea.

Downstairs Sean was also drinking from a steaming mug sitting on the settee where he had spent the night. Katey had made it clear that he was welcome to share her bed, but he had not pushed the issue. It was work time and Sean did not mix business and pleasure. It could wait, Sean was certain that he would be lying by Katey's side for many nights to come. Sean threw back the blanket and headed for the kitchen, he was still fully dressed. A quick rinse of his face and he headed upstairs to Ralph.

Sean knocked on the bedroom door – which seemed strange to both men – Ralph was still sitting up in bed eating his breakfast, and quite enjoying the comfort.

SCAPEGOAT

'We'll be off in about half an hour, you'll have lot's of time as the old man will start fishing about half a mile above your position.'

'Right, I'll be down in a minute.'

'You'll be getting three rounds, one for each bodyguard and one for the target.'

'I'd prefer four, then if it goes wrong I'll have one for myself!'

'Don't you be worrying about that, they'll not be arresting anyone, not today. I will be staying up there with you, in the pick up position, if anything goes wrong I'll have you out of there soonest'

'And from there?'

'From there we come straight back to the cottage, you are taken back to the city by Quigley. It's easier to hide you in the city, I'll follow with the woman.'

'What about the security forces?'

'They'll have enough on their hands, there's another diversionary shoot in Ballymena and a small bomb in Larne. After the past months of peace there will be chaos.' He handed the three rounds over to Ralph, who in turn placed them on the small bedside table. Sean returned downstairs.
As he walked into the kitchen Katey turned to face him.

'It's happening today is it?'

'Yes, it'll be your last day here, back to your home and your girls. I promise.'

'I believe you Sean, I believe you.' She kissed him on the forehead.

'There's one more hurdle though.'

"Quigley?'

'Yes, Quigley he is due to arrive here later and pick up yer man after he has done the job. Don't worry though, use the gun if you have problems.'

'I can't though can I, the girls.....'

'We'll find the girls. Don't you worry. I'll let you know as soon as I find them.'

Sean had no quick fix, no solution, he just hoped things would fall into place. He could make Quigley talk, eventually, but time was against everything. Katey was safe, but she was caught in the quandary; play Quigley's game or risk never seeing the girls again. Why? Why had she got involved she thought to herself as she packed her personal clothes in her bedroom. The Brit had left the house and was checking his kit for the job, outside in the shed. Sean walked into the bedroom, put his arms around Katey's waist and whispered over her shoulder.

'It will all be okay, I'm sure. Trust me.'

'I do trust you Sean, it's not you that's the problem.'

'I've spoken to the boys watching the Murph, they are confident he will show today.'

'You go on Sean, you have work to do. I'll sort out Mr Quigley if he gets out of hand.'

'You be careful.' With that Sean managed one of his rare shows of affection and planted a quick kiss on Katey's neck.

Ralph had checked all his kit, cleaned the three rounds of ammunition and put the rifle in the grip. He stood waiting as Sean came out of the cottage.

'All alright?' He enquired.

'None of your concern, you ready?

'Yes, as ready as I'll ever be. Let's get it done.'

Both men got into the vehicle, Sean did not look back as he drove down the track.

—-oooOOOooo—-

SCAPEGOAT

The Patrol stood waiting by the heli pad for the arriving of the Lynx helicopter, Steve turned to Andy who was unusually quiet.

'Don't worry it'll work it self out, these things do.'

'Aye,' replied Andy, 'if it's left to us it will, but that bastard TS will stick his spoke in given half a chance.'

The helicopter arrived and sent dust flying into the air, the Patrol ran forward half dragging their heavy bergens with them. Andy stood by the door and helped each one of his patrol in turn, finally accepting a helping hand himself. Within seconds the helicopter rose from the compound and disappeared from view.

Within minutes the city streets below gave way to the rolling green countryside. The plan was for the helicopter to head north towards Larne, then west following the coastline. Helicopters in the sky over the province had been an everyday sight for many years, this one would draw no adverse attention. Once over a more isolated area the aircraft landed, briefly, it's occupants exiting in seconds and heading into the waiting woods and gullies. The helicopter would then continue on its original route for several miles before making a detour back to base, avoiding the target area. At staggered intervals over the next few hours more patrols would be dropped in their chosen locations by the same method. The patrol sat in silence for a while watching and listening for a reaction to their abrupt arrival in such a tranquil place. No reaction; Andy nodded, the nod was passed on and slowly the patrol pulled on their backpacks and followed their leader as he picked his way up the wooded hill, his HK53 rifle at the ready.

Over an hour later the patrol approached its destination,

a small copse that would be used as an observation post for the next few days. Once secreted in the trees Andy and Steve took up watch, the other two relaxing to their rear, laying back on their packs face up to the sky catching the flittering spring sun as it to penetrated the young leaves. Steve used the radio to establish communications with headquarters and the other four patrols that were positioned about a mile apart. This done, at a whisper, he sat facing backwards as Andy searched the ground to their front with his binoculars. They were on a bank that overlooked a meandering river that was making its leisurely way to the sea. Apart from a few sheep grazing in the distance all was quiet, in fact tranquil. They settled into a routine, after an hour or so Steve would take his turn on the bino's, several hours later the pairs would change positions. Ears and eyes were wide open, every slight noise investigated.

Back at headquarters Captain TS studied the large map on the wall, he had plotted the positions of each patrol and was deep in thought. He still had not taken over his new post and his predecessor was in charge of this operation. He was frustrated, an ideal chance to make his name and he was stuck in the Ops room.

'I do think I should have taken command on the ground, we don't know what situation they will be confronted with.'
He talked to the map, aiming his words at the other Officer.

'I could be on the edge of the area in a position to support the patrols or move them about if necessary?'
The other Officer tried to ignore him and made no comment.

'After dark I could resupply them, anything! I can't just sit here all night.' The other Officer had had enough of him.

'That's your job out here I'm afraid. The Close Observation Platoons are covering the approaches, the Det will react to any sightings and follow them in and the Troop will carry out any executive action. You sit and wait.'

The phone rang and the officer embarked upon a long-winded conversation with a staff officer who also wanted to be involved in the action.

'Hello, call sign three, this is zero, radio check. That's difficult.'

'Problems?' TS asked the Signaller.

'Yes Sir, OP three have a duff radio.'

Capt TS thought for a moment, the other Captain was still engrossed on the phone.

'Tell them to be at the RV in one hour, I'll take out a spare.' Capt TS walked briskly from the portacabin, he had found his plan of escape.

—-oooOOOooo—-

Quigley eventually surfaced leaving last nights female conquest snoring like a pig in the grubby bed. He cleaned his teeth in the usual manner, gargling the flat lager before spitting it into the sink full of dishes. With his work head on he headed out into the street.

'Standby, standy, that's Alpha Two from Charlie one and right.'

The observation post had waited patiently for a sighting, the cameras clicked as Quigley walked up the street. At the top he took an unhurried left, for all his faults he was a professional terrorist and showed no signs of being aware.

'X Ray has, still foxtrot on the left.'

The Operator sat reading a newspaper in the old rusty saloon car, as he transmitted the sighting. Quigley crossed the road and walked up a wide alleyway running behind the terraced rows of houses. He was followed by a youth on a motorcycle, the Operator moved his position to keep eyes on the target, as he drew level with the alley way he just caught sight of Quigley cocking his leg over the seat of the bike.

'It's a pickup, Alpha Two is on the motorbike!'

The six man team closed in, attempting to cover all the exits from the alleyway. The youth on the bike knew his stuff, up one alley, across the street, into another. Within minutes he had changed general direction and was half a mile from the surveillance team. At the back of a betting shop the bike drew to a halt, Quigley walked off without a word and got into a parked car. Within seconds he was heading out of the city. Forty minutes later as he sat at a set of traffic lights he reached for his mobile phone

'All quiet, yes, it better be. Them kids okay are they? Good. Yes today's the day, you keep a low profile. Yes. Tonight, they're your's tonight, but not until then, I'll ring you later and give you the score.'

Had he bothered to look to his left he may have seen a motorcyclist talking into his helmet.

"Stand by, stand bye. Alpha two sighted at orange four"

Almost as soon as he was sighted he was lost again. A motorcycle is too obvious when trying to follow a car closely. But it was an important sighting, it narrowed the target area and confirmed they were in the right place.

Even if he was a murdering animal the other man's fascination with young girls disgusted him, but he owed the Tout's wife and he could not think of a better way of hurting her. In the flat in the Ballymurphy the two girls were becoming irritable, the younger one had cried constantly for the last hour, they

SCAPEGOAT

both sensed things were coming to a head. The evil man was nervous, sitting opposite them with a strange smile on his unshaven face. He cursed as he opened the cigarette packet, no fags, no milk or bread. He screwed up the empty packet and threw it towards the girls.

'Shut your bloody sister up before I shut her up!'
The older girl put her arms round her sister and tried to comfort her, but the younger one could feel the fear and cried even louder.

'You two keep quiet, I'm off out to the shops soon, keep quiet and I'll buy you some chocolate, okay?'

Neither girl acknowledged his peace offering.

—-oooOOOooo—-

Drop off complete Ralph stood in the woods putting on his camouflaged jacket and loading the rifle. He stashed his bag under a pile of pine needles and dead branches and slowly made his way towards his firing position. Sean had revered the car into a gap in the wood several hundred yards from where Ralph had disappeared into cover. He didn't like having to stay in the area, especially with a vehicle, but Kelly had been insistent. 'Keep your eyes on the Brit' he had said, 'one wrong move and finish him.' This was more a job for the likes of Quigley. 'When the job's done see to the Brit, make no mistakes!' Sean was not happy with his lot today, not with the fact that Quigley would be arriving at the cottage any minute and he had not heard from the boy's in the Murph. Sod it, he snapped, there was no way he was going to let Quigley have a go at his woman. He would sort him if necessary, he quickly removed the branched he had draped over the car and started the engine. Ralph stopped and turned at the sound of the engine, that was not the plan, but after a moments thought he continued on his way.

—-oooOOOooo—-

Back at the cottage Quigley was parking, he also had taken all the back roads and avoided the eyes of the Det. He had stopped at a public phone box in a quiet village; his call had only taken seconds. Katey stood in the kitchen watching her enemy as he stretched after his journey. No call from Sean, the girls, no answers. Control of her destiny was slipping from her. Quigley walked in.

'Hello sexy, thought you would at least have a brew ready for your man?'

'Fuck you Quigley, where's my girl's, are they safe? You will rot in hell if as much as a hair of their head has been touched.'

'That's no the way to talk to the man who controls all that is precious to you is it?'

Quigley walked over to her, grabbed a handful of red hair and twisted her head to face his.

'Remember, you be a good girl and you'll have your girls back safely tonight.'

He then planted a deep kiss on Katey's lips, forcing his tongue deep into her mouth. She knew it was impossible to resist as she was pulled by her hair into the front room. God, she wished the phone would ring.

—-oooOOOooo—-

Sean had thrown caution to the wind and was bouncing the car down the track at a ridiculous speed, a cloud of dust

SCAPEGOAT

following the erratic route. Avoiding a large boulder in the middle of the track he managed to slide the vehicle into a deep, muddy groove. The car swerved to the right, the back wheels sinking into the mud. He accelerated, but only bedded the car deeper.

'Bastard!' He kicked the car.

—-oooOOOooo—-

The empty cigarette packet hit the back of the unlit fire.
'You two, keep quiet. Don't go near the door or you'll not be seeing yer mommy again yer hear?'
The frightened girls just nodded acknowledgement. The door slammed as the man made his way to the corner shop for his cigarettes, the girls hugged each other as if to celebrate his departure.
'We're in business, there's the bastard now.' The men watching the shop pulled on their coats as they hurried from the flat.

—-oooOOOooo—-

Katey looked down as Quigley lowered his head, he was even attempting to be gentle, nibbling at her nipples through her blouse. She looked to her right, the cigarette box that contained the Walther pistol. Underneath the cushion she had hidden the knife, if only the phone would ring, if only. Quigley had pulled up her skirt and was burying his head between her legs, she felt sick.

—-oooOOOooo—-

Sean had given up trying to free the car from the mud, it was all going wrong. He took a snap descision that defied his usual cold professional approach and started running down the track towards the cottage. Logic went out the window he knew Katey was in danger and for once in his life he put someone else before the cause. With long strides he ignored the slippy ground and dodged the large stones, every second counted, somehow he knew that much.

Quigley had finished his meal and licked his lips as he sat back up next to his victim. He raised his buttocks as he undid his flies and took himself out, he intended to fully insult Katey today. She pulled back but Quigley grabbed her by the hair again, pulling her down towards his groin. Again, she was trapped. Again, she had no alternative as she accepted her fate and carried out his evil wish. Quigley looked down, the usual evil smile across his face.

'Come on Touts wife, take it all you bitch.'

Katey had tears streaming down her face as she reluctantly carried out the sordid task, out of the corner of her eye she could see the handle of the knife protruding from it's hiding place. Quigley loved the feeling of power and could not resist a comment.

"Looking down at the back of your head reminds me of the night your Liam begged for mercy. He didn't get any either."

In an instant she snapped and seemed to go into automatic pilot pulling Quigley towards her. Quigley mistook the action as a change of heart, closing his eyes with the pleasure of his total domination. Katey's right hand found the handle of the knife without searching, in a second she had turned her head, grabbed Quigley's manhood and sunk the point of the blade deep into the base. Quigley let out a scream that initially took his breath away; a split second later he looked down at the pool of blood forming in his lap. He screamed in rage releasing a punch directly into Katey's face, she fell backwards but at the same time pulled the knife upwards slicing Quigley even more.

She lay half-conscious, blood running freely from her mouth, the knife still in her hand covered in blood.

'Suffer, you bastard.'

Blood sprayed as she spoke pointing the knife at his face. Quigley bent over his injury in absolute agony, but he found strength from somewhere and kicked out sending the knife flying across the room, with another lunge he grabbed the bleeding Katey by the throat. She fought, but her efforts seem to have no effect on her assailant as he choked the life out of her. In desperation she reached out towards the small table and the cigarette box that hid the gun. Even at full stretch the tips of her fingers were still a foot short of their goal and she was losing consciousness. Her children were reaching out for her, giving her hope, giving her strength. With a final spurt of effort she reached forward again, this time managing to push Quigley slightly backwards. Her fingers touched the small table cloth and she started to gently pull the material, inch by inch towards her. Finally her knuckles felt the wood of the cigarette box, with a last pull the box came towards her , falling from the table to the floor. A quick search with her open hand located the handgrip she searched for, a moment later a loud, crisp bang and Quigley fell backwards into the pool of his own blood, still with the same sickly smile fixed on his face. Katey collapsed onto her side, the effort, the shock, all too much for her.

On the hill to the east all the patrol looked towards the sound of the gunshot, without a word of command they made to advance to investigate. Steve held the handset of the radio up questioningly to Andy, who shook his head in answer. One after another they followed Andy across the field at the half run, leaving their heavy backpacks secreted in the copse.

Sean stopped in his tracks when he heard the shot ring out, he was close now but was he too late. He slowed to a cautious walk as he entered the yard, with his pistol at the ready he approached the back door.

'Katey, you all right? Katey!'
Without waiting any longer he swiftly entered the house, covering himself as he passed any doorways. The sight that confronted him at the front room came as a shock. Quigley was half sitting on the floor, head back on the settee, motionless. He sat in a pool of deep, dark blood a trickle could be seen oozing from a hole in the side of his head. No longer a threat.

Katey, was she alive? Sean walked slowly, hopefully across the room towards her. He knelt in front of her fearing the worse.

'Katey?'

A tear inched its way down his right cheek as he reached out to hold her.

'Sean, Sean, the girls?'

'Don't worry yourself, as long as you are alright. One thing at a time.'
He held her close as they sat in silence.

CHAPTER SEVENTEEN

The elderly man was enjoying the days fishing, he had hooked one but the fight had only lasted seconds before the salmon slipped the hook and headed downstream to freedom. He had not been upset. He had caught many such fish over the years and in fact had lost several similar one's. At the moment he was casting across the falls; the water cascading six feet or so before crashing loudly into the boiling pool. Any outside noises could not be heard over the roar of the waterfall, including distant gunshots. Having covered the pool the angler made his way downstream, casting as he progressed.

Ralph caught the movement out of the corner of his eye, firstly one of the bodyguards high on the opposite bank, then the target engrossed in his fishing and finally the other bodyguard walking slowly some distance behind his master. He pulled his camouflaged hat down as far as he could without blocking his view, his breathing was steady and a bead of sweat inched its way down his forehead over the camouflage cream. The rifle was at his shoulder. Already the cross hairs of the telescopic sight were trained on its target.

JAMES RHYS ROBERTS

—-oooOOOooo—-

Captain TS had delivered the new radio to the patrol but had then hung around in the general area, ignoring radio messages from his fellow officer to return to base. He responded immediately to the report on the replacement radio of a gunshot in the distance, with a brief look at the map he gunned the engine and sped off. As he drove towards the area he wondered why the nearest patrol, Andy's, had not reported the incident, but he was not surprised.

—-oooOOOooo—-

Sean held Katey tightly, she was sobbing uncontrollably. Slowly he managed to walk her out to Quigley's car, away from the blood and gore in the sitting room. He left her and quickly returned to the cottage, setting about the task of removing what evidence he could. Katey had packed all her belongings and all surfaces had been wiped and bleached, but Sean knew that a few fingerprints or fibres would remain to entertain the Scenes of Crime Officers. He entered the front room and took a long look at Quigley, no pity for him, Quigley deserved all he got. Sean took all the belongings out to the car, returning with a large can of petrol and a box of matches.

—-oooOOOooo—-

The men in the Murph had to be careful. As a colleague their faces were obviously known to the pervert, and even though he was a pervert he was also a terrorist and would be

SCAPEGOAT

watching out for anyone watching him. Especially now. As he left the shop he quickly scanned the area but failed to notice the man in the telephone box. He hurried back to the flat and the girl's, it would all be over soon he hoped. Turning the key in the lock of the flat door, he turned as he caught the slightest sound behind him - too late, the pistol caught him hard across the back of the head. His world turned black and he fell to the floor.
Both girls screamed as the men entered the room.
 'It's alright my young friends, we're the good guys. We'll have you back with your Ma as soon as we can.'
The girls smiled nervously. The man dialled the number into the mobile.

—--oooOOOooo—--

Sean was busy splashing petrol throughout the house when the mobile rang, his face lit up and he almost ran out to Katey.
 'Thank God! Yes darling, I will be with you soon, you just do what the nice men tell you. See you both soon.' She handed the mobile back to Sean.
 'Well done and tell the men thankyou. Yes, yes, get the girls back to their Nan's and then give the bastard the good news, and don't be worrying about Quigley, he's history.'
 He snapped the phone shut and smiled at Katey who was beginning to calm down. At last things were starting to go right. Sean returned to the cottage and took great delight in splashing petrol into the still smiling face of the dead man.

—--oooOOOooo—--

JAMES RHYS ROBERTS

The angler inspected the small fly on the end of his line, he carefully checked that the points of the treble hook were still sharp. Satisfied he continued casting down and across the river with the long split cane rod. The two bodyguards looked across at each other confident in their coverage, just another day. The ratchet on the fishing reel sang out as the line straightened across to the far bank the rod bending against the large salmon that had taken the bait. Without panic the experienced fisherman started winding slack line back onto the reel, this done he set about landing what felt like one of the better fish. It took many minutes but eventually the silver fish was at the angler's feet, with a skilled hand it was grabbed by the tail and half carried, half slid onto the bank. He didn't often kill his fish these days, but this time he dispatched his vanquished quarry with a swift blow of the priest. Holding the fish high he sent a big grin across the river to his long serving bodyguard, who was also an accomplished fisherman.

The capture of the fish had caused the elderly man to walk even further down the river and he was now only thirty or so yards from Ralph's position. After lowering the fish gently to the ground the angler put down his rod and bag and turned towards the bushes. Slowly he walked directly towards the sniper's position. Some six feet from the muzzle of the rifle he stopped, looked casually about and unzipped his fly. 'Too close' Ralph thought to himself. 'I'll get him on the way back'. The sweat was streaming down his face, his breathing quickening as the adrenalin flowed.

'I don't know who you are, but get on with it if you must.' The words took Ralph by surprise.

'I've had a perfect day, caught my last fish – I'm as ready as I'll ever be to meet my maker.'

SCAPEGOAT

Ralph raised himself onto his knees, the rifle still pointing at its proposed target; the final decision. It was made and Ralph stood up, turned around and walked back through the bushes towards the woods. Not another word was spoken. Suddenly a shot rang out. The man across the river had seen it all, identified the weapon and the threat, and even though the enemy was now walking away had made up his mind to assist. The round hit Ralph high on the left shoulder sending a chunk of jacket and flesh flying into the foliage, the force of the impact pushed him forward onto his knees. His instincts and training came into play and ignoring the pain he adopted the prone position, in an instant he had his sights trained on the security man and without hesitation made his reply. It hit the large man in the centre of the chest. Further pistol shots came from the other man on the riverbank but Ralph was back on his feet and running fast towards the woods, back to where he had left Sean. The elderly politician had remained cool throughout the incident, but without any warning clutched at his chest and fell to his knees. The surviving bodyguard cancelled any pursuit and attended to his boss.

The four-man SAS patrol had observed the brief incident as they moved in to investigate the first shot and Andy led them through the woods with caution. Ralph leapt the fence but landed in a heap, his wound was burning, he could have screamed with the agony. In his mind he recalled the words of a fallen comrade he had protected in Coleraine hospital some years previously.

'Its all right being shot, but no one mentions the pain, it's like having red hot pokers pushed through you.'
He was right. Ralph wanted to throw away his rifle but his soldiering instincts told him not to. He pushed hard through the

trees into a small clearing and took a rest, falling to his knees. The blood flowed freely down his arm and dripped off his fingers.
'Stay perfectly still!'
Ralph recognised the voice immediately.
'Put the rifle on the ground and back off Ralph.'
'Okay Andy, I've had enough.' Ralph did as he was ordered, the four man patrol emerged from the trees, guns at the ready.
'How did you get yourself into this mess, they must have had some hold on you mate?'
'It's hard to explain, I was low, really low, the drink and all. Then, my kids. I wasn't thinking straight. I am now.'
'Bit late to get your shit together, the world's been mobilised to get you.'
'Well, in a way I'm glad its you mate, I can imagine your orders. Get on with it.'
Andy said nothing, after a short pause he picked up the Woodmaster rifle.   'You've been hit, Bob get your pack out and stop the bleeding.'
Bob quickly took a field dressing from one off his pouches and started to dress the wound.
'We can help you a bit, but at the end of the day you'll have to escape on your own, and without this.' Andy shouldered the rifle and looked through the sights at the ground.
'Getting soft are we Sergeant Woods?' No one had heard Captain TS come through the trees. He pushed his way into the clearing, his MP5K sub machine gun at the ready.
'Screwing the nut for your old mate is it? More like disobeying orders I believe.'
'No Sir, nothing that you wouldn't do for one of your mates...'

SCAPEGOAT

'You should know by now Woods, I do not have any mates. Now stand back and you stop dressing that wound it will be wasted effort.'

'But Sir,' Andy protested.

The Captain made no reply but aimed his weapon directly at Ralph, his thumb could be seen pushing the safety catch onto automatic. Ralph closed his eyes in expectation. A single shot rang out.

Ralph opened his eyes just in time to see the Officer land on his back, a split second later the sub machine gun landed beside him. If he had landed in a hospital he would have been declared dead on arrival. Andy stood firmly, the Woodmaster rifle in his hands and a wisp of smoke spiralling from the barrel.

'As I was saying, we'll help you as much as possible but it won't be easy. In addition now you have just killed a British Officer!'

Bob was back at Ralph's side dressing the wound.

'We will give you as long as we can then report a sighting to the north. Later we will discover the Captain's body. Sorry mate that's the best we can do.'

Ralph got to his feet.

'Thanks, I couldn't ask for more.' Ralph turned to the rest of the patrol. 'Thanks lads, one day, God willing I will repay the debt.'

Andy walked forward and gave his mate a hug, being careful not to cause him any pain.

Without further words Ralph turned and left.

—-oooOOOooo—-

Sean walked briskly from the cottage, into the car and

drove down the track; Katey turned her head towards him and managed a smile. A second later there was a muffled explosion and a large plume of smoke rose into the air above the cottage. Sean put his foot down, they still had the problem of getting back to the City.

—-oooOOOooo—-

As night closed in the sky was alive with helicopters and searchlights, their thick beams of white light penetrating every suspected hiding place. Ralph had made good progress despite having to make several detours in order to avoid uniformed army and police checkpoints. Luckily the many valleys and wood lines gave him cover from view. Now he would have to watch out for the thermal image devices both on the ground and in the air. His arm was now less painful, the dressing had been expertly applied. He was convinced he was out of immediate danger and was being more careful in his route selection. Where to go? What direction had been the initial problem, but he had made his mind up to head west then south, over the border. He had no money, no clothes as such and no idea what the future held but the constant thoughts of his children, and the risks Andy and his patrol had taken for him kept him going. He had a future; he knew he had.

He was in his element, escape and evasion, avoiding capture at all cost; another military game. Ralph made good time, taking the risk of running along the edge of fields when he felt safe. As dawn broke Ralph drank enough water from a stream to replenish the liquid the wound and the running had drained from him and he was now sleeping under a pile of dead branches deep in the conifer forest. His mental plan was set; lay up

SCAPEGOAT

by day, make ground at night. Food would have to be found tonight, even if it was only turnips put out for the sheep. In time he needed to find a change of clothes, but that could wait a while. He intended to cross the border as soon as possible then slow down a little. How he was going to get out of Ireland remained a mystery.

—-oooOOOooo—-

Sean continued to bounce the car from one track to another, avoiding the main roads totally. Within ten minutes he was driving through the open doors of a large barn and parking next to small saloon.

'Sean, I have one question.'
'Does it have to be now, we need to get away from this area.'
'Was my husband a tout?'
The depth of the question shook Sean, he wasn't expecting it.
'He said he was, admitted it apparently. I wasn't there but I've spoken to those who were.'
'In your opinion then, what do you think?'
'In my opinion. Liam had taken a beating that would have killed most men, he was adamant that he was true to the cause. It was only when you and the girls were threatened that he cracked and agreed to anything that was said.'
'I thought so, and who shot him?'
'I think you know the answer to that, and you have just paid him back, so let's put it all behind us, we've got the girls.'
Katey was crying again, sobbing. Sean put his arms around her and held her tightly.
'Yes, you are right.' She wiped the tears away and forced

a smile.

As per the plan Sean got into the boot of the car and within seconds Katey was at the wheel driving down the lane to the main road. After only a mile she encountered the first of several vehicle checkpoints, but having been waved down she was waved on again without coming to a halt. No one was looking for a woman on her own, 'but there could be someone in the boot' she thought to herself as she continued on her way. Some miles on she was stopped by a patrol, this time she was allowed on her way after a few simple questions, the young police officer did not even ask to see her false driving licence.

As she entered the city she calmed down, she was back on her own turf. After parking the car on a back road she and Sean made their way to meet the girls on foot. Approaching the house they noticed a man across the road, one of the lads who had found the girls, he nodded the all clear. Katey pushed open the front door of her mother's house and almost ran inside, the girls saw her and screamed in delight. All three stood in the centre of the room hugging and crying.

'Mommy, you won't leave us again, will you?'

'No my darling, never, ever again.' She ran her fingers through her youngest daughters hair as she spoke, the tears rolling down her face.

'We didn't like that horrible man, mom. He smelled and had green teeth.'

'He didn't do you any harm, did he?'

'No mom, he was just not nice.' The older daughter was no longer frightened of the man.

Sean walked across the room and put his arm around Katey.

'I'll be off now, things to do.'

'You'll be back though?'

SCAPEGOAT

'Yes I'll be back, then I'll not be going away again.' He gave his woman a long loving, kiss. Her mothers smile lit the room.

—-oooOOOooo—-

Andy had taken initial command of the scene. Now, with the outer cordon in place, the area taped off and the scenes of crime officers going about their business in their white disposable over suits, it was time for the patrol to return to base. They had run quickly through their story but were still nervous about the interrogation they were destined to be subjected to. The helicopter approached from the south and they made their way reluctantly to the open field. A police officer ran up to Andy and spoke in his ear, he in turn turned to the patrol and smiled.

'The old man had a heart attack, he didn't shoot him at all!' Andy had to shout the news over the noise of the landing Lynx. All smiled in return, the injuring of a bodyguard would not be investigated with as much vigour as the murder of a prominent politician. The search for Ralph would probably lose momentum once the news got out. Once loaded the helicopter dropped down the hillside before gaining height and returning southwards.

—-oooOOOooo—-

Kelly sat in the big leather armchair, his attention was riveted to the screen of the extra large television. On the screen, pictures of the police and the army charging the rioters bought perverse pleasure to the ageing schemer. Unexpectedly Sean walked into the room. He had bypassed all the alarms and stood, gun in hand, facing his boss. Kelly continued to watch the television showing no sign of surprise or fear.

'Well that was a fuck of a job.' He got up from the chair as he spoke.   'Good job our Prot friends know what they are doing, this Drumcree rubbish is winding them up into a frenzy.'

Kelly poured himself a large brandy. 'Care for a nightcap?'
Sean shook his head.

'No, no thank you. We need to talk.'

'Need a gun to talk nowadays, do we?' Kelly nodded towards the pistol pointed at him.

'No, I don't need a gun. In fact I never want to touch a gun ever again, here.' Sean threw the weapon onto the carpet.

'Go on then me boy, get it off your chest.'

Sean moved forward and dropped into the chair facing Kelly.

'I've had it. Finished.' He leant forward, elbows on knees, head in hands.

'You know as well as I do, you don't retire or resign. Not from this trade.'
Sean rose to his feet and walked slowly round the room.

'Is this your part of a free Ireland? Come on, you retired years ago. Greed, cunning, crime and profit, and more profit, that's all you want.'

'Don't be so narrow minded, you have worked hard for all this. It's about time you started to share in your success.'
Sean rounded on his former boss.

'No, no Mr Kelly, I want none of your spoils. I want my life back, my freedom. I've lost my Country, not to the Brits but to the likes of you.'
Kelly bent down and picked up the pistol. Sean looked at him in disgust and shook his head.

SCAPEGOAT

'Go on then, use it if you can, if you are capable. When did you last kill a man? If ever.'
With that Sean made for the door, not rushing, expecting the worse. As he reached the door Kelly spoke.
'Sean, as far as I am concerned you have served your time. I admire you, always have. Go in peace, but watch out for the men from Dublin, they may have a different attitude towards all this.'
Sean didn't reply, he just turned to leave without any show of emotion.
Kelly sat for a short time sipping at his brandy, he reached for the telephone.
'Pat, we need to talk, work to do. Yes, you. You have been promoted. Tomorrow. Usual place, usual time.'

CHAPTER EIGHTEEN

The noise from the props changed tempo as the heli started its descent into the camp. Andy could clearly see the welcoming committee lined up facing the landing pad. The Commanding Office and Regimental Sergeant Major from Hereford, the Troop Commander and several others he didn't know. He wished he could slip the pilot a tenner and get him to take them somewhere else, but it was time to the face the music.

As the engine of the aircraft died, the patrol grabbed their kit and made their way over to the welcoming commitee.

'Sgt Woods!' The Commanding Officer walked forward as he called out.

'Yes Sir.'

'We need to talk, all your patrol okay?'

'Yes Sir.'

'The RSM will talk to them briefly.' The Officer gestured for Andy to leave his pack and led him some distance from the others.

'Woods the Regiment has lost an Officer. Why?'

'Sir?'

'It is no secret that you and the Captain did not get on, and I am not suggesting any foul play. The whole incident just doesn't ring right.'

'I couldn't agree more Sir. What I want to know is what was the Captain doing in the area and why weren't we informed of his location. Yes Colonel, I have as many questions as you have.'

The Commanding Officer paused, deep in thought.

'Yes Woods, there are many questions, but at this moment we have two dead bodies and one injured bodyguard. One by natural causes, the other two with gunshot wounds. Also an assassin on the run.'

The Colonel was attempting to piece a jigsaw together, but Andy was hiding a few of the pieces.

'Woods, you are now to make a statement to the police.'

'Yes Sir.'

'As far as I can fathom out you and your patrol saw nothing, heard the shots and found the bodies. The only witness is the surviving bodyguard who also says he saw very little.'

'Right Sir.'

'You obviously realise how sensitive this incident is so I think you may find that the whole thing was a regrettable accident. Following the reports of a threat, your patrol, commanded by Capt TS was deployed. The dead bodyguard over reacted, the politician couldn't take the excitement and the other man saw very little, or will say he saw very little.'

'But Sir.'

'No Sgt Woods, no but's. Understand?'

'Yes Sir, I understand.'

Both men walked back to the main group, in the background

SCAPEGOAT

stood two CID men waiting to take statements from the patrol. As Andy picked up his pack the RSM helped him with one of his shoulder straps.

'Good job Andy, very good job. The Regiment is a better place today.'

Andy turned and made eye contact.

'I'm sure I don't know what you are talking about RSM.' He allowed himself the slightest of smiles as he spoke.

—-oooOOOooo—-

That night Sean held his woman tight. There was no sex. It was not necessary. All that would come with time and they had plenty of that. What Katey needed now was security and compassion, and that was what she would get. There would be no turning back, he could not imagine living without her, not now. Why had they wasted all those years?

'What happens next? I don't want the bastards to come in the night for you, I couldn't stand that again.'

'No, we'll be off. How's that sister of yours in Canada? Fancy paying her a visit, for good?'

'Yes, yes I do. Sean?'

'Yes.'

'I love you...'

They held each other closely and drifted off into a heavenly sleep.

—-oooOOOooo—-

Two weeks later, on a dark wet night on the dockside in Dun Loaghaire a figure could be seen skulking in the shadows.

Ralph had been lucky, he had stowed away aboard a livestock truck not knowing where it was heading. He and the sheep had sped through the night, over the border and into the free state. From there he had made his way carefully on foot towards the port. Accumulating clothes along the way he now looked half-presentable in a donkey jacket and jeans. The wound had been clean, and after an initial period when he thought it had become infected it had started to heal.

He watched as the two drunken sailors boarded the rusty old container ship. Ralph could not recognise the language, eastern European he thought but wasn't sure. Moments later he followed their route up the gangway, turning left and heading for the shadows once he was aboard. He had salvaged two loaves from a bin behind a local bakery and had two large pop bottles full of stream water. Enough for a few days, after that he would have to come out of hiding. He felt quite comfortable laying full length in a lifeboat. Within minutes he was sound asleep.

During the night, he didn't know what time, Ralph felt the vibrations of the huge engines starting. He stayed in his hiding place, drifting in and out of sleep. An hour or so later he could feel the bumping of the ship leaving its berth. He allowed himself a sneak, last look at the emerald isle. He had gone through a lot and come out the other side virtually unscathed, he swore then he would never allow himself to be as down as he had been. He thought of his children, would he ever see them again?

As he drifted back to sleep he promised himself two things. The first was that one day soon he would return to see his children. The second was that one day in the future he would have a little word with a certain Mr. Kelly.

SCAPEGOAT

—-oooOOOooo—-

The Commanding Officer sat in the plush office of the Commander Land Forces, Northern Ireland. To his right was the man in the suit from the government.

'So, we still do not have the ID of the assassin, nor any sign of him.'
The Lieutenant Colonel was summing up his debrief.
'And Captain Thackray-Smith?' Enquired the CLF.
'Yes, I know what you mean, didn't quite ring true did it.'
'The assassin, wish we knew who he was, we could use a man like that.' Added the suit.
The CLF stood up marking the conclusion of the session, he offered his hand to the SAS man.
'Jeremy, it's all ended in an acceptable manner, pity we lost one of our better informants; Quigley was useful at times. But please keep your ear to the ground a secret is no longer a secret when you have told one person. The truth will leak out one day.'
'Yes sir, I will do just that.'
'Have a good journey back to Hereford and give my regards to your wife; I'm off to Drumcree to take stock. Becoming an annual outing, damn marches.'
'Well I suppose they keep the bowler hat industry going.' Quipped the suit as they walked from the office.

The End